RECKLESS
Kiss

RECKLESS

Kiss

AMELIA WILDE

CONTENTS

PROLOGUE

Dominic

W*HAT IS EVERYONE ELSE GETTING OUT OF THIS?* The heated thought scorches itself into my soul like the tropical sun that's beating down on the white sand beach, and I shift in my lounge chair, shaded by an elaborately patterned umbrella. Turquoise ocean waves lap rhythmically at the shore. I lift my feet from where they've been buried in the sand underneath the chair and brush them off. I feel like an idiot in this pair of bright lime green swim trunks, one of ten bathing suits my staff stocked in the master suite closet of my elaborate vacation home.

I'm not going to go swimming. Odds are, I'm not even going to take off the white t-shirt I'm wearing with the trunks.

I take another bite of what's supposed to be lunch. It's something delicate and fruity—the chef is one of the best in the British

Virgin Islands, if not in the world—but every bite I put in my mouth reminds me of chewing Hawaiian Punch–flavored cardboard.

My phone sits silently on the table. I'm supposed to be on vacation from Wilder Enterprises for three whole weeks—the first vacation I've been on since taking over the reins of my father's company six years ago, after he made an absolute disgrace of it—and my executives have been strongly encouraged to forget that my phone number even exists for the duration of my stay.

My jaw clenches at the interminable, abysmal silence. I'm already regretting agreeing to take this vacation *and* issuing that order. Without any emails and texts coming in, I have no earthly idea what's happening at the company while I'm away, and...well, I need to make sure everything is running smoothly.

Not keeping a close eye on everything, my thumb on the pulse, is the kind of thing that sends businesses right off the rails. It sure as hell happened with my father. He let things lapse. He seemingly disappeared for an entire year, only checking in at the office every now and then it seemed, as he took one expensive vacation after another and started pursuing a bunch of birdbrained hobbies, dragging my mother all across the planet, from one destination to the next, and before you knew it, Wilder Enterprises was hemorrhaging out of control, losing contracts, its reputation, everything he had worked so hard for all these years.

I wind my fingers around a narrow, sturdy glass filled almost to the top with something sweet and light and alcoholic, but I don't take a sip, instead simply staring at the contents.

"You don't look like you're enjoying yourself."

I look up into the pale blue eyes of a lithe blonde woman with enormous tits, and I dismiss her callously before she can speak another word. I can tell by the barely-there bikini, the sarong tied suggestively around her waist, that she's the kind who wants to weasel her way into my life by promising that it will only be a fling, but then she wants *more,* and before you know it, you're calling security to have her dragged off your property. A thousand dollars says she's renting one of the expensive vacation residences along the beach.

I'm never going to see her again, so I tell her the truth. "I'm not."

A smile perks at the corner of her lips. It does nothing for me. She'll be here or somewhere like it, trolling endlessly down a beach, long after I'm gone, looking for a prize. "I could help you with that," she breathes out seductively.

I give her a tight-lipped smile. "I'm sure you could." Then I stand up from my lounge chair, taking the glass with me. "I have to go."

She pouts a little, and her eyes narrow as she looks me up and down. "Stay...with me." Her hand is moving toward her neck, toward where the bikini is tied in the back, casually, like she's going to make it look like an accident.

A cold wave of anxiety sweeps through me then, rocking my heart back into place. I can't stand the silence of the phone, the lack of communications, the creeping sensation that things are slipping out of my grasp, like I might come home to news like I did last time, when my mother committed suicide. I feel like one more false move might send someone else careening over the edge. My father's the only one I have left. We hardly ever speak, after what he did, sending the company into an abyss so that he could *enjoy* himself...

Jesus.

I have to get out of here.

I turn away brusquely from the blonde, stalking up the beach toward the house, already firing off messages to my driver, to my pilot—an emergency call to get things packed up and moving. I want to leave within the hour.

I've been on vacation for three days, but it's all I can take.

Vivienne

My desk phone bleats from the corner of my desk. Its belligerent tone hammers against the wall of concentration I've built, allowing me to focus intently on wrapping up my latest case. I've spent a good hour longer than I should have fine-tuning the summary presentation for my boss, but I want it to be perfect. I'm on the verge of accomplishing something great at the FBI, creating a career and a name for myself in the Bureau that my parents will be proud of, but more importantly, one I want so badly I can taste it.

"What's up?" I say into the phone, still trying to surface from the depths of the summary.

"You working on something?"

"Just finishing up the summary for the Christiansen Inc. case."

"Leave it, and come to my office."

My boss, Milton Jeffries, clicks off the line without saying another word. My heart beats fast in my chest as I shove my chair away from my desk. The urgency in his voice tells me this is something new, something big, something I could hang my hat on.

When I knock at his door, he's hunched over his keyboard, as usual, his salt-and-pepper hair impeccably styled and his suit neatly pressed, the very picture of a detective from the old noir films, even though he's somehow firmly rooted in the present. "Sit down," he says without preamble, and I drop into the seat across from him. "I need you on a new case. Hand off the summary to somebody else."

"But—" I've put a lot of blood, sweat, and tears into this thing, but I bite back the rest of what I was going to say. Going to battle so I can finish up some paperwork is *not* how I'm going to climb the ladder here...and I've already been climbing at a record pace. No reason to derail my progress now. "What's the case?"

Milton pushes a folder across the desk toward me. "Wilder Enterprises."

"Never heard of it."

"You wouldn't have. They deal in energy technology, and they're like this with the government." He wraps two fingers around each other in a symbol of tightness. "Sensitive information, going both ways."

"What's the deal?"

"Someone's stealing their tech secrets and selling them out to a contact in China. It might be the Chinese government."

"Shit."

Anything involving the illegal transfer of information between someone in the U.S. and the Chinese government would be a big, nasty deal—something *way* over my pay grade—and I instantly understand why as I scan over the contents of the folder, names and dates rolling along...until I see the picture.

"Who's *that*?"

The man stares seriously out from the image, blue eyes blazing even in the still-life picture. That is one *cut* jaw.

Milton cranes his neck. "Dominic Wilder. He owns the company, and he's still in the dark about all of this. He has to be, because we don't know yet if he's involved."

I give a low whistle and flip the page, even though I want to keep staring into those eyes for the rest of my life. "Got it."

"Review the materials and get back to me by the end of the day with any questions. You start early next week as an employee in one of their departments—it's all in the folder, along with your undercover identity." Milton says briskly. "And Viv?"

I look into his eyes, my hands tightening on the folder. "Yeah?"

"I don't have to tell you this, but—"

"This is an important one."

One sharp nod, and I'm dismissed.

My heart pounds in my chest as I make my way back to my desk. This could be *it*. This could be the case I've been waiting for—the one that will make all my years of hard work worth it, the one that will wipe away all the angry sneers and comments from the men who didn't want me spending so much time at the office, the one that will make me into the kind of woman who doesn't need a man for anything.

All the years I've spent alone and lonely will finally pay off.

It will have all been worth it—worth it to land this one case.

CHAPTER ONE

Vivienne

*D*on't drop the doughnuts. Don't drop the doughnuts.

With every precarious step I take down the New York City sidewalk, the thought repeats over and over again in my mind like the dumbest mantra I've ever heard. Even if I *do* make it to the office without dropping these damned doughnuts, I can tell that the phrase will have lodged itself in my mind and stick there for days, maybe even weeks.

This all started out as a relatively simple idea: bring in treats on my first day at the office to endear me to everybody in my new department—the *Executive Support* department—at Wilder Enterprises, my employment home for the foreseeable future.

It got *complicated* when the June weather turned upside down, whipping itself up from a calm and pleasant—though slightly overcast—day into a voracious thunderstorm when some rogue cold front smashed into the steamy heat rising above the city early this morning. I woke up to the sound of raindrops lashing against my window ledge, and I promptly snuggled deeper into my pillow.

Rain like this means there are no cabs. No cabs means I have to take the subway. The subway means having to walk three blocks carrying an enormous box of freshly baked doughnuts.

The box wasn't meant to be *this* big, by the way. I was going to bring in a respectable two dozen, and if my department turns out to be bigger than that, well, tough luck. But the guy selling the doughnuts at the cute little family-owned bakery three doors down from my apartment had to be so *nice.* He gave me a big grin, flashing his white teeth and prominently displaying his dimples, and insisted on throwing in another dozen, artfully arranged in a box so big I ended up taking two seats on the subway.

I shrug one shoulder upward, trying to hoist my purse strap up farther on my arm to keep it from slipping down. It's a constant struggle, what with the bulky raincoat I'm wearing in what turns out to be a futile effort to keep my clothes dry. The collar of the neat and professional suit jacket I'm wearing underneath it is soaked—I can feel it—and one of the buttons near the throat is coming undone. Correction, it *is* undone, which means the front of my silk shirt is—

Well, I can't think about that now. The effort it's taking to bring in freshly baked treats on my first day of work, not to

9

mention doing so through a rainstorm, will no doubt endear me to my future colleagues, if nothing else. It's hard *not* to like someone who shows up on the first day bearing doughnuts and wearing a wet shirt, looking slightly sheepish and green behind the ears.

It's going to be seen as a nice gesture, even if it's only an illusion. I've pulled it off so many times before, and every time successfully.

Today might be the first time my entry into a company like Wilder Enterprises goes totally off the rails.

I take a deep breath, tightening my grip on the unwieldy box of doughnuts. It will definitely be the first time I've worked an investigation at a company even *remotely* close to the size of Wilder Enterprises. So regardless, this is a whole new ballgame. Although the stakes *would* be a lot lower if this was only some annual sporting tournament that goes on to affect almost no one. Instead, this is my big chance to prove myself at the FBI.

You can do this, I remind myself without the slightest hint of irony. It takes some serious cojones for a woman with no experience beyond a journalism degree with a focus on investigative reporting to do *anything* in the FBI, but I've managed to pull it off more than once. For five years, I've done...well, not to brag, but I've done rather well for myself.

But it's time to move up in the world, and Wilder Enterprises is how I'm going to do it. All I have to do is conduct this investigation exactly by the books. No funny business, no getting attached to anyone at the company—none of that. It's cut and dried: I need to get in, get to the bottom of what's happening, and get out, hopefully with a big fancy medal waiting for me back at the home offices.

Not literally. But if it's in the form of a pay raise, I'd certainly take it...

I shake my head to gather my thoughts, a scattering of raindrops falling from my hair. The torrents of rain continue driving down around me, mixing with the downpour battering the streets and any sidewalk not concealed under the protective covering of an awning.

I still have a block to go with the dampened cardboard box of doughnuts getting heavier by the minute when the wind starts to pick up.

No, no, no. I tense myself, bracing myself against the sheets of wind. The last thing I need right now is for a howler to come racing between all the skyscrapers and upend the giant pink box I've been clutching in my hands for most of forty-five minutes.

Picking up the pace isn't an easy prospect, what with the slick sidewalks and the stilettos I've chosen to wear today, quite the combination considering the weather—I should have gone with the kitten heels—but I do my best, taking smaller steps and *hustling.*

"Vivienne Davis," I say under my breath, keeping my tone bright and even, just how I will speak when I enter through the doors of my newest place of employment for the first time and introduce myself. I've spent the last few weeks securing my undercover identity. Vivienne Davis is close enough to my real name that I won't forget it, but if you look up Vivienne Davis, you won't find even the tiniest clue linking it to a woman who works for the FBI. All you'll discover is just a few random and well-placed tidbits about little old me, a graduate of NYU and former executive assistant at Farwell Limited, a company based in New Mexico that has all the makings of a real business without actually *being* one.

That was my idea—the fake business, just in case anyone in the HR department at Wilder Enterprises went to the trouble of researching my background. I doubt they did—most organizations of this size don't actually bother aside from the basics—but you never know. It's always better to be safe than sorry.

Only half a block to go.

The towering skyscraper that houses Wilder Enterprises headquarters *has* an awning, though it doesn't span the building's entire front face, just the area directly over the entrance.

Just get to the awning. And don't drop the doughnuts.

I'm almost there. I'm going to make it. I'm *so* going to make it that I'm almost home free.

Ten steps. Five. Three.

With a little whoop of triumph that I mostly manage to keep contained under my breath, I take the final step, putting me firmly—and safely—underneath the awning. The final step—the one that actually hides a crack in the sidewalk.

The heel of my shoe slips perfectly into the crack... and snaps off like a twig.

The sidewalk is *just* damp enough that even though I try to balance myself, even though I try *hard,* I can't quite get purchase with my other foot. My right knee twists painfully as the heel gives up on its last inch of life.

I lose my grip on the box—then catch it again—but I'm still falling, and—*shit*—the street has suddenly become a giant wind tunnel, right now, right at this moment. The gust of wind coupled with the driving sheets of rain are so strong that it *whistles* as it seizes the clear lid of the box. I scramble to slam it down back into place, but too late I catch sight of the horrible angle of the box—too late to stop the jelly doughnut that was perched right on top from flying out and right into the opening of my raincoat, smashing its innards onto what had been until seconds ago my neatly ironed white shirt.

My knee slams down onto the concrete, putting an end to this embarrassment, and doughnuts go scattering in all directions. There are only about a dozen survivors, and then there is me, kneeling on the sidewalk, my knee throbbing in burning pain, the heel of my right black stiletto broken, the raincoat hood blown off my head, while a car—black and sleek and by the looks of it *way* too expensive for me to ever dream of owning—glides up to the curb just in time for whoever is inside it to witness the whole thing.

The driver hurries out, bustles swiftly around the side of the car closest to the awning, and pulls open the back door on the passenger side, standing aside for a tall, elegant man who is so gorgeous that he must be a descendent from some kind of Greek god to step out onto the sidewalk. He fixes his flashing blue eyes on me, and then his lips appear to dip into a frown, just a little.

I have to choke back a gasp. He's *that* sexy.

Worst of all, I recognize him.

My embarrassment is just beginning.

CHAPTER TWO

Dominic

I HAVE NO IDEA WHY THIS WOMAN—*THIS* WOMAN, WITH HER emerald green eyes that are so vivid they're almost glowing, even in the dreary gray backdrop of the storm, curves so fine I can trace their lines even under the black raincoat she's wearing, and the most perfect damn lips I've ever seen—is walking in the rain carrying an absurdly large pink box of pastries.

If the events of the last few seconds haven't made her ask the very same question, I don't know what will.

I looked up from the deluge of emails I'd been scrolling through on my phone just in time to see her go down hard, the hot pink box slipping and shaking in her hands, and by the pink color in her cheeks, she must know I witnessed the entire thing.

She looks up at me from her awkward position on the sidewalk, her lips parted slightly, and I'm at a loss for words.

A man in a sallow-colored trench coat comes up behind her, shouting into his phone. "*No,* you asshole." His voice is nasal, high-pitched, and it sets my teeth on edge. "I told you to move that product or find yourself another job. If your desk isn't cleaned out by the time I get there, I'll kill you myself." As he snaps angrily into his phone, he registers there is a woman splayed out on the sidewalk and steps gingerly around her, his belittling and condescending expression implying he's sidestepping a steaming pile of garbage. My jaw clenches tight.

I don't really have time to perform a rescue mission, even if it is happening right outside my office building, but something about her has arrested my attention. Stopped it dead, right in this moment, and I can't act like that prick on the phone. Not this time.

So even though I have a meeting scheduled with some of my top executives and only about five minutes to prepare, and even though I *called* the meeting, I do the only thing I can think of.

I step over to offer my hand to help her stand up.

"Are you all right?"

At my words, her face flushes from pink to scarlet. "Yeah. This is the best day of my life." Her tone is rueful rather than biting, and she hesitates for a moment before she reaches up and puts her hand in mine. A *zing* dances up my arm, zeroing straight to the middle of my chest, and she takes in a quick little breath.

Our eyes meet for another eternal second, and then she drops her gaze, grasping onto my hand a little tighter as she pulls herself up.

When she does, she's not quite steady on her feet. "*Shit*," she says softly, and her face turns an even deeper shade of red. "Sorry."

"Do you have an extra pair of shoes?" It's an idiotic thing to say, and 1 know it, but 1 have to say *something*, and her hand in mine is leeching all of my cool business demeanor right out of me. I'm actually finding it hard to breathe.

She flicks her eyes upward, catching herself just in time. "No. And now my doughnuts are all over the ground." She squares her shoulders, seeming to will herself to gather her composure. "Well, thanks for the hand up. If you could just forget that you ever saw this—"

"Not a chance."

She shoots me a dark, but surprised look. "Why not?"

1 don't know what it is—if it's the storm, if it's the way she looks, the tendrils of her dark hair escaping from the careful knot at the nape of her neck—but the next words that come out of my mouth are the pure, unvarnished truth. "You looked so good, kneeling down on the sidewalk."

Jesus. This is *not* what 1 had in mind when 1 stepped out of the car.

Her mouth contorts, and then she presses her lips into a thin line, nodding as if all of this is predictable, commonplace, disgusting. "1 think I've got things from here."

She's pissed, and as she stoops to pick up the box, which is now only about a third full of pastries, my brain works overtime to figure out what the hell to say to fix this. In this moment, I hate myself. Dominic Wilder, billionaire and president of Wilder Enterprises, the man with all the answers—and what, I have *nothing*?

"I'm sorry," I finally say, as she wrestles the top of the box back into place. My voice is low and urgent—*far* more urgent than I meant for it to be—but there's no way I can let her walk away from me like this. "That was inappropriate."

Her face shifts again, and she seems to make a decision, nodding once, sharply. "It was." Then her expression softens. "But we can just agree to forget it."

It's been a long time since anyone spoke to me in such clipped tones, and it's making me—well, surprisingly, not pissed, like it should.

"Is there anything—?" Christ. I have no idea why I'm pushing this hard, for some random woman on the sidewalk who I've never seen before in my life and will probably never see again. "Do you need a ride? To a shoe store, maybe?"

This makes her smile, at least a little, though there's a look in her eyes that I can't quite place. "No, actually." Her eyes flicker down to the sidewalk, then back up to meet mine. "I'm actually going in here. It's my first day at Wilder Enterprises."

I laugh out loud. "Oh, really? What department?"

She bites her lip. "Executive Support."

"I'm Dominic Wilder."

I didn't know a person's face could get so red, despite the fact that she was firing snippy responses at me just a minute ago. She sighs a little. "I know. I've—I've seen your picture."

"I look a little different in the flesh."

She screws up her mouth into one of quaint disgust. "I hate that expression." Then she remembers herself—remembers that I'm her new boss's boss's boss's boss. "I'm sorry. We're not getting off to a very good start."

"We can agree to forget it," I say, because when I look into those eyes, which are already burned into my brain, into my memory, it takes me a glacial moment to think of anything else at all. Except, of course, the *very* inappropriate things I'd like to do with— "What's your name, Miss—"

"Vivienne," she says, without hesitating. "Vivienne Davis."

"Well, Ms. Davis, you've having a *very* interesting first day."

"I wouldn't mind if the rest of the day was far *less* interesting."

"I'm sure that could be arranged."

Vivienne laughs, the sound uncertain. "I'm not—you're not firing me right now, before I even start, are you?"

"This *is* a place of important business matters," I say, eyeing the spilled pastries. "But I think we can let this one slide."

Let this one slide? Who the hell am I right now?

"Thanks." Vivienne's smile is small, tentative, and then she squares her shoulders again. "Well, I should—I should go in."

I offer her my arm. "Let me at least get you to the elevators in one piece."

Her eyes go from me to the box of doughnuts, and then she shrugs, turning the box on its side and tucking it under her arm like a briefcase. "They've already been dropped once." Then she slips her hand into the crook of my arm. At her touch, I feel a jolt pass through my entire body that warms me.

Three wobbling steps and we're inside the expansive lobby. Vivienne takes it in—the three-story atrium, the wide marble staircase leading to a second-floor restaurant, glassed-in elevators. "Wow."

"Welcome to Wilder Enterprises," I tell her. Even though the words are on the tip of my tongue, I stop myself from spilling out, *Don't ever leave.*

CHAPTER THREE

Vivienne

DOMINIC DOES EXACTLY WHAT HE SAYS HE'S GOING TO DO—he gets me to the elevator, wishes me good luck on my first day, and is gone before the doors slide closed.

I have ten floors to get my heart back under control.

Dominic is *not* the kind of man I typically go for. The kind of man I go for—when I have time, which is not that often, not in this line of work—is gentle, sensitive, and...

Boring.

It's like a shock when the word comes to me, like cold water trickling down my back. But that's not right. They haven't been *boring*, exactly, just...

I give my head a little shake, trying to clear the thoughts from my mind. Thankfully the elevator doesn't make any more stops, and by the time the doors open on the tenth floor, I've *almost* managed to make myself forget his blue eyes, clear like tropical water, the strong, sexy cut of his jaw, covered with stubble that looks meticulously maintained and rugged at the same time, the way his expensive custom-designed suit moved with a body that I'm absolutely positive is powerfully muscled and chiseled just like his jaw. I had to pretend to be disgusted at his comment, pretend it offended me. I'll never be able to admit that the sound of his husky voice sent tremors of desire pivoting to my core.

I've almost forgotten.

Almost.

There's a little reception area immediately off the elevator, and I step toward the desk, taking in a deep breath to steady myself.

The woman sitting behind the desk looks me up and down, and a wave of dark hair cascades over my face. The jolt I got when I put my hand in the crook of Dominic Wilder's arm rendered me pretty much senseless on the elevator ride, and now I feel like a living fun-house mirror. My hair has to be a mess from the rain, and I've got an enormous half-empty box of doughnuts tucked under my arm. I'm carrying my heels in my other hand. And—*shit*—there's got to be jelly filling staining my white shirt. Just about the only thing I did was to undo the raincoat, which has left my disheveled appearance entirely exposed to the woman behind the desk, who looks like she just stepped off a runway at New York Fashion Week.

This is *not* the way I was hoping to start my time here. Not at all.

I stand up as straight as I can, trying to will away the color from my cheeks. "I'm Vivienne Davis," I say, my voice sounding a hundred times more confident than I feel. *Play the part, Viv. No other choice now.* "It's my first day."

She raises her eyebrows, and I can practically hear what she's thinking. *It's your first day, and you couldn't even come in with a clean blouse?* But when she answers, her voice is cool and professional, even helpful. "Why don't I show you to the restroom before I take you back to meet Ms. Lillianfield?"

This receptionist might be a judgmental bitch, but at least she keeps it mostly to herself. I can't help but feel grateful. "That would be great."

She rises gracefully from the chair and holds out her hands. "I can take that, if you'd like."

"They're for everyone to share," I say as I awkwardly shuffle the box into a more normal position and place it into her hands. "There used to be more, but I fell on the sidewalk, and then there was a car—" *What the hell is happening to me?* I never babble like this, and I shut my mouth before Ms. Runway Receptionist actually rolls her eyes. She slides the box onto the surface of her desk and comes around to where I'm standing, cocking her head to one side.

"The restroom is this way." Of course, her outfit is also flawless—a navy skirt suit with a champagne-colored shell underneath, matching stilettos, and a delicate silver necklace that hangs gently around her perfect neck—and I look like a clown.

She steps away, leading me to one side of the reception area and down a discreet hallway, one tall door on either side. We're almost to the door when she says, over her shoulder, "I'm Portia, by the way. Welcome to Wilder Enterprises."

"Thank you. It's nice to meet you."

She nods like she's a queen, and *naturally* it's nice to meet her, and then she pauses in front of one of the doors. "The restroom is in here. I'll be back at my desk when you're ready."

Five minutes later, I emerge with at least some of the jelly doughnut remnants dabbed away from my shirt, my hair in some semblance of order, and looking a little bit less like a ragamuffin. My knee still throbs painfully from where I smashed into the concrete—my pantyhose are ruined—but at least I'm not actively bleeding. I've also broken off the other heel by wrenching it clean off the shoe. My heels are now flats, but at least they're the same height.

Portia gives a little nod of approval, and I'm almost overcome by the urge to tell her that I'm an undercover agent, damn it, and I far outrank her. But I just smile when she says, "Ms. Lillian-field is ready for you," and follow her back past some groupings of cubicles to a glassed-in office where a woman with black hair scraped tightly into a bun at the nape of her neck frowns at me from where she's sitting behind her desk, her back straight and her expression stern. Portia is gone before I know it.

"Ms. Davis," she says, standing up and extending her hand. I give it a confident shake as her eyes travel down the length of my shirt. It's not like I could get *all* the jelly filling off, and she clearly notices it. "I take it you had some difficulties this morning."

I smile and shake my head, trying to project an aura of assurance even though I'm off-balance, even though the memories of meeting Dominic Wilder are somehow still throwing me for a loop. "Just a little. I brought in doughnuts for everyone, but some of them became casualties of the weather when I had an...um... accident on the sidewalk."

Ms. Lillianfield frowns. "How nice of you." Her tone says anything but.

Okay—time to move on from the small talk, because clearly she's not going to be won over by my natural charm. "I'm *very* excited to get started." I resist the urge to cover up the jelly stain on my shirt with my hands, resist the urge to turn around and walk back out of here and tell my superior that this job is a disaster already and that nothing is going according to plan.

But damn it, I'm going to see this through if it's the last thing I do. I am *not* going to lose my standing in the department over a few lost doughnuts and a banged-up knee. I'm not even going to lose it over a chance encounter with the owner of the company. It's not like I'll be seeing him much while I'm here anyway, a thought that gives me an unexpected pang of disappointment.

"Of course." Ms. Lillianfield gestures toward the door. "I'll show you to your desk, and Marie can help you get up to speed."

I get my very own cubicle, and Ms. Lillianfield gives me a cursory rundown of the computer system, the items in the supply cabinet on the other side of the space, and the hours I'm supposed to be here—in a shocking twist, it's from nine to five—and then she turns and goes back to her office with a sniff.

I can hardly help letting my shoulders sag the second she's gone, but the relief only lasts a moment.

"Oh, my God, it's *you*!" The chirping voice belongs to a red-headed woman poking her head around the side of the next cubicle, and my gut goes cold. Is my cover already blown?

"It's me," I say lamely, covering it with a laugh. "Wait—do we know each other?"

"I'm Marie!" Her brown eyes dance with delight. "I saw you downstairs. *You're* the new girl?"

"Ha—yes." Oh, thank God.

But Marie isn't done. "I saw you with Mr. Wilder." Her voice is low, confidential, bursting with curiosity. "How did you pull *that* off?"

My entire body goes hot at the thought of him, of his eyes on me, of his hands on me. "My name's Vivienne," I say, giving her a pointed look and a little grin.

She covers her mouth with both hands. "I'm so sorry. I'm just—" Marie fans herself. "Let's get started, okay? You can tell me about Mr. Wilder later."

She launches into an energetic tour of the scheduling system we're going to use to assist the executives, and I follow along, my heart beating hard in my chest.

Forget him, I tell myself.

No. No. *No,* beats my heart.

CHAPTER FOUR

Dominic

Vivienne Davis is the last thing I need right now.

I don't need any distractions. I definitely don't need any women hijacking my brain, burning into my consciousness, and making my cock harder than steel and causing a tent pole in my pants. That kind of shit doesn't end well for anyone, if my father is any indication. It might not have been my mother who distracted him into losing everything, but after that embarrassment—after she died—

I wanted to push her into the elevator and hit the emergency stop button, trapping us between floors long enough for me to take off her absurd raincoat, lick whatever sweetness is left from the pastry explosion off her neck, and then, when she's panting breathlessly in my arms, let the elevator continue up past the eighth floor Executive Support department all the way up to the top floor, where I keep a private apartment for emergency purposes, like if I don't feel like calling for a driver to go back to my penthouse on the Upper East Side, or one of my friends needs a place to crash...none of that shit matters. What *matters* is that there's a bed up there, comfortable as hell, and I'd like to spread her out on it.

But I don't do any of that.

I escort her coolly to the elevator, letting her look all around at the elegant lobby of the building for a few moments, and then I turn and walk away the second she steps into the elevator.

One more moment of looking at her and God knows what would have happened.

The side effects are inconvenient enough as it is. Around the corner from the regular elevator is a private elevator exclusively for my use. Wilder Enterprises isn't the only company in the building—there's no way, with the level of intelligence flashing in her eyes, that she couldn't figure that out by herself—-but I didn't mention that I own the entire space.

The private ride up to my office suite gives me just enough time to adjust my erection.

I don't have time to think about her—I need to focus on the upcoming meeting, which is scheduled to begin in ten minutes. I need status reports from everyone at the executive level, and I'm not willing to wait.

I let out my breath on a deep exhale. They were probably

looking forward to the fact that I was going to be out of the office for the next three weeks, but I'm not at all sorry about ruining that for them.

I was *supposed* to be on vacation—my first real vacation since I took over the shattered remnants of Wilder Enterprises more than six years ago. In those days, they snickered behind my back. I know the kinds of things they said about me. *Any son of Peyton Wilder is already a failure. He's too young and stupid to manage a corporation of this size, with stakes this high.* "These stakes" did prove to be a challenge—government contracts for cutting-edge energy technology, for one, and complicated relationships with a number of suppliers and partners around the world—but I gritted my teeth and pushed away everything else to repair the company.

And repair it I did.

No thanks to my father.

I push Vivienne Davis out of my mind, burying her as deep as I can.

Focus.

I was supposed to be on vacation, and I couldn't fucking hack it. Three days in, I ordered that my private plane be prepared to take me back home. The property in the British Virgin Islands is nice enough, but it turns out that if you work for six straight years, there's not much waiting for you when you decide to take a break.

Not that I need anyone.

I don't.

Wilder Enterprises is more than enough of a companion for me.

But two days of sailing, two days of sitting in the shade on the back porch watching the ocean sparkle for miles, was enough to make my skin itch, and I needed to get back to work. I couldn't shake the feeling that it was all slipping out of my hands.

So I canceled the three-week hiatus from the office and came back.

To find Vivienne Wilder kneeling on the sidewalk in front of my building.

I clear my throat, even though there's nobody in the elevator to hear me, and wrench my thoughts away from her.

She's just another woman working at my company. That's all. Nothing more.

The elevator lets out a soft tone and the doors slide open to reveal a carpeted hallway leading into the study just off the main room of my office. The carpet muffles the sound of my footsteps. The closer I get to the office, the taller I stand. When I pull open the door again, I'm back to being the Dominic Wilder who rules meetings with an iron fist, the Dominic Wilder who nobody would ever dare snicker at again—not if they wanted to keep their jobs, which they all desperately do. The men and women on my executive team are paid handsomely. They don't want to lose all the benefits that Wilder Enterprises has to offer.

My personal secretary, Emily, is setting a tray down on the mahogany expanse of my desk when I open the door. She doesn't jump at the sound, just looks up at me with an even smile. "Welcome back, Mr. Wilder."

"Thanks, Emily. Is everything in place for the meeting?"

"Yes, of course. The beverage selection is out—would you like me to call down for any other refreshments?" Emily is blonde, and she has a pleasantly round face that never lets anything show, and her poker-face is part of why I chose her to be my secretary. Everyone who represents me needs to have a good grasp on what they show to the world, and she does.

She just happens to be the opposite of Vivienne Wilder.

Her name flashing across my mind again is followed by a spike of irritation. I *cannot* lose control of myself because of a chance meeting with some *woman* I'll likely never see again.

But I could, because she's down on the eighth floor, walking around right now with those emerald green eyes, that soft voice...

"No. No other refreshments."

Emily gives a nod and goes back out the door to the reception area, and I sit down in the executive chair behind my desk—top of the line and meant to be imposing—and survey the tray.

She's brought sparkling water and a bagel, meticulously spread with a thin layer of cream cheese, just how I prefer. I sip the water, but I can't bring myself to eat. All of my muscles are tensed, on edge.

I stand up and stroll over to the window with its view of Manhattan, obscured by the storm that's still thundering through the city, filtering everything in shades of dark and darker, and wait for my mind to quiet itself.

It might be shitty outside, but down on the eighth floor, there's a bright pink box of pastries and a woman with vivid green eyes, flashes of color to drown out the dreariness of the rain.

CHAPTER FIVE

Vivienne

Aᴛᴇʀ ᴍʏ ᴅɪsᴀsᴛʀᴏᴜs ꜰɪʀsᴛ ᴅᴀʏ, I ᴅᴏɴ'ᴛ ʜᴀᴠᴇ ᴍᴜᴄʜ ᴛɪᴍᴇ to dwell on Dominic Wilder—Dominic Wilder, the smoldering hot billionaire whose eyes lit my nerves and senses on fire—while I'm at the office.

For two reasons.

For one, the team at headquarters doesn't *think* he's involved in the transfer of information from his corporation to unfavorables in China. My supervisor, Milton Jeffries, specifically asked me not to concentrate my efforts above the executive level. As far as I can tell, Dominic is the only person that high up in this company. Of course, they couldn't give me—or anyone else at the FBI—any guarantees, which is why I'm here undercover and not as part of a cooperative effort with Wilder Enterprises. It's unorthodox for sure, but if it turns out he *is* involved—well, that's above my pay grade.

Secondly, there's barely enough time in the day for me to win back all the respect I lost by walking in here with a jelly doughnut smeared on my shirt. It's a damn fine line. I can't be too much of a standout, because once I'm done with this job, I want to fade out of people's minds, leaving me free to pursue other cases. But I need to be perceived as trustworthy so that I can move up the ranks, at least a *little*, and gain access to the kinds of information that will tell me what I need to know.

Just what that information is, I'm not sure yet.

But I throw myself into my job, which is like being on an entire team of secretaries. For the first two weeks, they book me solid with the kind of minutiae that I can tell usually goes to the greenest people on staff. I double-check itineraries for executives traveling to various events and conferences and meetings around the globe. I file expense paperwork. I double-check the expense paperwork that other people file. And then I refile it.

Two weeks and one day after I start at Wilder Enterprises, I'm double-checking more double-checked expense filings, really getting into the flow, half starting to wonder if being in Executive Support is my true calling in life instead of working for the FBI, when Ms. Lillianfield's terse voice breaks into my thoughts.

"Ms. Davis." I swivel around in my seat, a prepared smile on my face. "Am I interrupting?"

Well, yeah, but if this is my big break— "Not at all. I was just coming to a stopping point. What can I do for you?" I stopped saying "what's up?" after four days at Wilder Enterprises. Ms. Lillianfield is the gatekeeper, that much is clear, and she is surprisingly old-fashioned for a woman who works for one of the world's biggest energy companies. The slight downturn of the corners of her mouth told me she hated "what's up," so I scrubbed it from my vocabulary, along with "hey" and "no problem."

She considers me for a moment or two, taking me in from head to toe. I've started to subtly mimic her style, which usually consists of a smart skirt suit and hair played up in a tight bun. I see a flash of approval in her eyes when she gives the bun in my own hair a cursory glance. "You've been doing well here." Approval or not, her voice is still a little begrudging. I incline my head and wait. Ms. Lillianfield also doesn't like to waste time on pleasantries like being thanked for compliments.

Another long moment of appraisal. "In view of this, I'd like to reward you with a more complex assignment."

She sure plays her cards close to her chest. "I'd love to take on a bigger project."

Ms. Lillianfield gives me a sharp nod. "Wonderful. I'll send you an email in about ten minutes with all the details. Come to me if you have any questions." Her tone indicates that if I have questions, I'm *probably* not cut out for whatever this assignment is.

"Thank you, Ms. Lillianfield." By the time the words are out of my mouth, she's already halfway back to her office.

My heart beats a little faster in my chest. This could be it—this could be the sign that I'm starting to gain a foothold here, and then I can really get moving on this case. They'd be so damn impressed if I came in early and under budget on this one, and there'd be no stopping my ascent at the FBI.

I fly through the rest of the expense reports and wait for the promised email to come in, tapping my foot anxiously against the industrial carpet. Marie pokes her head around the cubicle wall. "Did something happen? I heard Lillianfield in here a minute ago."

"Just waiting on a new assignment." Her lips go into a round O, and I smile at her.

My computer pings—a new email has arrived—and I whip my head back toward the screen. It takes a second to load. "Come on, come on."

Ms. Davis—

I'd like you to coordinate a meeting for executives Feldman, Overhiser, and Childs with the individuals listed below at some point during the Mumbai conference next week. This will need to be slotted into available openings in their schedules, confirmed with all three of their staffs, and coordinated to successful completion...

I stifle a giggle at "successful completion," then force my face into a sober expression as I read the rest of the email.

This is it.

This *has* to be it, because there have been rumblings in the cubicle farm about Overhiser and Childs each posting and hiring for chief executive assistant positions in the next few weeks. There's no way this isn't a test to see if I'd be cut out for one of those jobs.

I can't hide a small smile of satisfaction from appearing on my lips. Despite everything, despite the torn pantyhose and the jelly doughnut stain, I'm making headway. I'm going to untangle this thing, and I'm going to do it in record time.

A note at the bottom of the email catches my eye. *Feldman, Overhiser, and Childs report directly to Mr. Wilder, who will have final approval over all negotiations made during this meeting. Please prepare a summary of the outcome and have it to him within twenty-four hours of the meeting's conclusion.*

My heart flies into my throat.

In the back of my mind, I knew that the executives at Wilder Enterprises would come into contact with Dominic Wilder. I just didn't think that making this leap would involve reaching out to him personally, even if it *is* entirely work-related.

He'll see my name on the summary that I send.

I shake my head a little. It's not going to make an impression on him. I'm undercover, for God's sake, and dropping that box of doughnuts was the last—and only—time I need to come to his attention.

He's probably forgotten about me already, I reassure myself, but deep down, I'm not entirely convinced.

CHAPTER SIX

Dominic

"MR. WILDER?" EMILY STANDS AT THE DOORWAY TO MY office, her hand poised to knock gently in case I'm buried in some work.

In fact, I am *not* buried in work. I'm staring out the window, taking in the Manhattan cityscape on a brilliant June day—and I'm thinking of Vivienne Davis.

I haven't seen her in over three weeks, not since she swept in on that storm and wormed her way into my mind, but more and more of my days have been devoted to imagining what she's doing. What she's wearing. How she's spending her evenings.

Now I'm caught by my own secretary, daydreaming about her.

I clear my throat and straighten my back, keeping my tone

light, keeping my voice even, like the thought of bending Vivienne Wilder over my desk hasn't preoccupied me for the last ten minutes. "Yes, Emily?"

"There's a Chris O'Connor on the line for you."

That name makes me perk up. "Chris O'Connor?"

"He said he was an old friend."

"He's not lying about that." I keep my face impassive, and so does Emily, but there's a tension in the air that I can't hide. So I decide to crush it beneath my heel and move on to the next moment. "Put him through."

"Of course."

It takes her a few moments to get back to her desk, and I stare at the handset in front of me. Chris O'Connor went to Yale with me, and now he's with the FBI. He's been with the FBI for seven years, just long enough to—

The phone beeps with the incoming call. I pick it up.

"Mr. Wilder, I have Mr. O'Connor on the line." Emily's voice is smooth, even.

"Thank you, Emily. It's been a long time since I've heard from you, Chris."

Chris waits a few beats for Emily to click off the call, and then his voice rumbles across the line. "Hey, Dominic." His tone is reserved, cautious, nothing like the college student who used to whoop and posture every time he scored in a game of one-on-one.

"You have some news for me?" I don't know what the hell

this could be about—nothing in my personal life this time, that's for damn sure—but Chris isn't the type to call and chat. He's too busy now, and so am I. We lived together for two years as college roommates. We don't have to check in often.

"Listen—" He hesitates, and my throat goes tight. This is *weird.* If Chris ever does call, it's to invite me out for a drink, and that happens on the order of once every couple of years when he's getting nostalgic about something.

"Spit it out, man."

He lets out a sigh. "Look, I shouldn't be calling." *Then why are you calling?* I want to ask the question, but I wait. "Are you free for a quick lunch? Or just a drink?"

Something tells me this isn't about Yale, or catching up.

"Sure. I can meet you in fifteen minutes. Where at?"

He names a bar a few blocks down from the Wilder Building. I hang up and feel a pit in my stomach.

* * *

Chris sits across from me at a back booth, hands wrapped around a cold mug of beer. He twists and turns his head, scanning the room, and then looks back at me. "So...how are things?"

I sip my own beer and narrow my eyes at him. "You didn't call me down here to ask me how things are, and we both know it."

His blonde hair is darkening with age, but it gives him a certain sophistication that he definitely didn't have in college. He takes another sip of his beer, then leans back and looks me in the eye. "I shouldn't be telling you this, but I just couldn't—" He shakes his head, looking pained.

I raise both hands into the air. "You don't have to tell me anything that's going to get you in trouble."

"Yeah, but—" He lets out a breath. "Okay. Listen. The department is investigating Wilder Enterprises."

I can't help but laugh. "For what? And why haven't I been notified?"

Chris drops his voice. "Economic espionage."

I glare at him. "Are you fucking with me?" It would be out of character for him, but this seems damn ridiculous. Who would be stealing from me? I have a vetting process in place at every level of the company, and I keep a tight grip on what goes in and out.

He doesn't look at all like he's joking. "No. Look—somebody is stealing your tech secrets and passing them off to a group in China. We're not sure if they're connected to the Chinese government, but—" He presses his lips into a thin line. "The investigation is undercover at this point because the team had...some suspicions."

It takes me half a heartbeat to understand what he's saying, and when I do, anger surges up into my throat. I answer him through gritted teeth. "If you're suggesting that I'm conspiring to benefit foreign governments, then—"

Now it's Chris's turn to throw up his hands. "*I'm* not. I've vouched for you. But this has been going on for a good three weeks, and I couldn't keep you in the dark about it."

I pull out my wallet, throw a bill that's far too large onto the table, and stand up. "I'll be in contact with someone at the Department. You can bet on it."

"No. Dominic—"

"What the fuck do you expect me to do, Chris? Just sit here and take it?"

"Give us a few more weeks," he pleads, his eyes wide. For an instant, I see him as he was at twenty years old, almost a decade ago now, the gangly kid on campus who everybody loved. "Just sit tight, Dom. I swear to you, we've got someone good on it."

They've gotten someone into the company under my nose, and Chris isn't about to blow his cover. My gut churns. I don't need this to go public about as much as Chris doesn't need to lose his job over leaking a confidence to an old friend. Still, my skin feels clammy. Someone inside Wilder Enterprises is fucking me over. I rule with an iron fist, and someone...*someone*...is wriggling through, passing off valuable information to a contact in China.

Jesus Christ.

Chris lowers his voice, trying to keep his cool. "A few more weeks. Just let the team have a little more time, and we'll figure it out. We'll have it shut down." He swallows hard. "I know it isn't you, man. *I* know that, and I have your back."

He's trying to do me a favor, and my old friend is risking his damn job to do it. The least I can do is give him what he asks.

"Fine." Chris's face relaxes. "But if this shit isn't resolved as soon as possible—and I mean *as soon as fucking possible*—there will be hell to pay."

"I know." Chris reaches for his beer, nods across the table to me. "At least finish your drink, man. You don't have to raze the city to the ground yet."

CHAPTER SEVEN

Vivienne

I RUB ONE HAND ACROSS THE BACK OF MY NECK, TRYING TO work out the knot with my fingers.

This job wasn't nearly the in-and-out production that I thought it was going to be, and the last ten days have been hell. It's at the point where I've almost stopped looking for Dominic's car in the mornings while I'm moving along that last block to the office.

It's been a long evening on the phone with people ten hours away in a different time zone, and my back aches from sitting in the chair. My eyes are dry and they ache behind the glasses I've been wearing instead of my contacts, and I'm starving—but it's over.

The project is *almost* over.

I searched out the perfect block of time in the midst of the three executives' tangled schedules, booked a conference room from halfway across the world, triple-checked the details with six different staff members, and even coordinated a meal to be delivered at the ideal interval for a break.

I lean my head into the phone, listening to the final few moments of the meeting. The words are starting to blur together—I've been up since five this morning—but the men's voices sound jovial, satisfied.

"Thank you, Ms. Davis." Mr. Childs' drawl breaks into my thoughts, and I bolt upright in my chair. "I think we're done here."

I'm damn proud of myself for not giving any sign of how unbelievably exciting this is, even though I want to leap out of my seat and jump up and down. "Wonderful," I say, keeping my voice neutral. "Is there anything else I can do for you, gentlemen?"

Overhiser says something in a low voice, but I catch the general tone of it, and the tone makes my skin crawl even from a continent away. The room around him is filled with chortling from the other men. The past ten days have given me a little window into what these people are like, and Overhiser raises the hairs on the back of my neck. It's a tingling sensation that tells me something's up with him. I let Jeffries know about it today, before the big meeting began.

"I have a feeling about him," I told my boss, stabbing my fork into the takeout salad I had for lunch.

"Do you have anything a little less cliché? Any solid evidence?" My boss laughed, his deep voice rumbling across the line.

"No. I just have the sense that I'm zeroing in on the inside contact." There's been some debate on the rest of the team about whether or not the information is being leaked by someone who infiltrated Wilder Enterprises from the outside, or someone who's been here all along, and the more time I spend on this project, the more I'd put my money on Mr. Overhiser.

"Follow it up, Viv," he'd said, and I heard the approval in his voice. *Follow it up.* I've done so whenever he's given me the green light, and it's served me well so far.

"That's all, Ms. Davis," Mr. Childs says once the background laughter has faded out. "The notes should be hitting your inbox any second now."

My computer pings at just that moment. "Confirmed. I'll have a summary up to Mr. Wilder in no time. Have a good flight back, gentlemen."

They sign off with a chorus of goodbyes, and then the line goes dead.

"*Yes.*" I punch my fist into the air, then sag back into my seat.

It's over—except for one thing.

The summary for Mr. Wilder.

Just get it done.

I desperately want to go home. I want to go back to my place—the only place where I can be my real self—and take a shower that lasts for a year, curl up in front of the TV with a bottle of wine and an enormous amount of sushi, and relax.

But that'll just put off this work until tomorrow morning, which will push back everything else I have to do, which will make it take one day longer to close this case.

I rub at my neck one more time, then straighten myself up in the chair, pull up the meeting notes, and glare at the screen.

It's probably the least taxing part of the entire project, but my hands tremble over the keyboard as I type up the summary, save it as a document, and attach it to an email.

Dominic Wilder has almost certainly forgotten about me by now. He might not be so forgetful when he sees my email signature at the bottom of the note.

Dear Mr. Wilder,

I pause, my hands loitering over the keys, and think of his eyes zeroing in on me in the rain, drinking me in, burning through me, that electric hum that raced up my arm when I put my hand in his, the way it felt to steady myself on his arm and breathe in his clean, spicy scent.

I've been meaning to thank you for—

I delete that line. *So* unprofessional, and I already did thank him. Didn't I? I roll my eyes. Dominic Wilder is not lying awake at night, three weeks later, thinking about how I didn't thank him for doing what any decent man would do.

I start again.

Please find attached to this email a summary of the meeting with executives Feldman, Overhiser, and Childs for your review.

So far, so good.

I'm available at any time if you have any questions.

I delete that line, too. Like he's going to have questions for *me*. This is *his* company.

I hope you find this helpful.

Delete.

It's late, and I'm tired. I bite my lip, trying to think of the right phrase to use. Finally, when a yawn takes over my entire body, I slam my hands back down onto the keyboard.

I'm happy to answer any questions about my work.

Best regards,

Vivienne Davis

Executive Support

Then, before I can think about it for another second, I hit send. The email goes on its way with a little *whoosh*.

I stand up from my desk, rising up on my tiptoes to stretch my calves, and then slip my feet into my high heels. Home. Home *now*. Then it's Friday, and then I'm going to spend all weekend reviewing case information, interspersed liberally with Netflix and popcorn.

I'm just putting my purse over my shoulder when my computer pings.

"No way," I say under my breath, and reach for the button on the monitor to put it to sleep for the night. It'll automatically log me out when I do that.

But the email sender's name stops me dead.

Dominic Wilder.

What the hell is he doing answering emails at ten o'clock at night?

My heart beats overtime, and both my hands tremble. I should go. I should just go, and check the email in the morning.

I can't do it.

I click the mouse furiously, opening the email, ready to be disappointed if it's an auto-response message, ready to pretend I'm relieved.

Ms. Davis,

Thank you for the summary. Are you available for a quick question?

Dominic Wilder

President, Wilder Enterprises

The next moment, the phone on my desk rings, shattering the silence enveloping the floor, and I give a little shriek, then get myself under control.

My heart in my throat, I snatch up the handset.

"Vivienne Davis."

"Ms. Davis." The voice on the other end of the line is his, unmistakably *his.* "It's very late to be in the office. I'd like to offer you a ride home."

CHAPTER EIGHT

Dominic

I REACT WITHOUT THINKING WHEN I SEE HER NAME ON THE email.

I've been in the office for hours, reviewing the final touches on a number of contracts—contracts I shouldn't even be spending my time on, but after the meeting with Chris, I've instituted a tighter review policy—and the emails stopped coming in a long time ago.

Until hers.

Vivienne Davis is sending me a summary of a meeting between three Wilder Enterprises executives and some potential partners for a massive deal in India, and damn, the woman is dedicated—because it comes in just after 10 p.m., when nobody in their right mind is still in the office.

Except for me.

It's a terse and formal note, with no hint of the spitfire attitude of the woman I found out on the sidewalk that day, but my mind doesn't linger on the professional office bullshit. All I see is the time stamp, and the image of her sitting downstairs at her desk, the image of her walking alone to—

To God knows where. I don't know where she lives, although I could always look it up in her personnel file. Is she going to get a cab, or is she going to walk to the subway?

Something rears up in my chest at the thought of her out there, alone, in the semi-darkness of the New York City night, and before I can stop myself, I'm typing up a reply, thoughtless, sending it.

The moment it's done, I know it's not enough. *A quick question,* Jesus. I couldn't care any less about the summary at this moment.

"Fuck."

I reach for the handset of my phone and dial in the number, hesitating over the extension. *What the hell is wrong with me?* I scroll to the bottom of the email with my left hand, punching in the extension as soon as it registers.

She answers on the first ring. "Vivienne Davis." There's the slightest hint of breathlessness in her voice, and it zings up and down my spine to hear it.

"Ms. Davis. It's very late to be in the office. I'd like to offer you a ride home."

I'd like to offer her more than that, but it's the first thing that comes to mind, and I have to do something to lower the chances of her walking out of here by herself.

She hesitates a beat. "Mr. Wilder?"

"It's me, Ms. Davis."

"You can—" I can hear her swallow over the phone. "You can call me Vivienne."

Heat spreads out across my chest. "Vivienne, it's much too late to be going home by yourself."

She laughs a little, the sound clean and pure. "I've lived in the city for quite a while, Mr. Wilder. I'm not afraid of the dark."

"Indulge me."

Her breath is soft over the phone, and I picture her with her head cocked to the side, considering. "Just as long as you don't think I can't handle a subway ride home. Even if it's past eight o'clock."

This is the kind of flirtatious talk that would never happen during the daytime, never happen during office hours, and it's like a spark that jumps from the morning three weeks ago straight to now, as if it's the very next day. She's holding her own. She's not giving in to me, at least not at first, and that's a rare quality in anyone who works for me these days.

"I'm sure you could, Vivienne." There's no mistaking it this time—when I say her name, there's a hitch in her breath. "But I'd like to see you safely home. Are you ready to go?"

"Yes, I am."

"I'll be down in the lobby in one minute."

"I'll see you there."

I hang up the phone and whip my cell out of my pocket, dialing for my driver. He responds with a clipped "right there, boss," and I know he'll be idling in front of the building in thirty seconds flat.

It's all I can do not to sprint to the elevator.

I haven't seen Vivienne in three weeks, and I'm starting to look for her in every woman I see on the streets.

I shouldn't be doing this.

I get into the elevator.

I shouldn't be doing this under *any* circumstances. She's a grown woman. She can handle getting home by herself. But more than that, she works for me. Any hint of impropriety—

But damn it, I'm going to. *I'm going to.*

The elevator lets me off at the same time the other one lets her out into the lobby, and for an instant I see her biting her full lip, head turning, scanning the area for me. The sight of her nearly brings me to my knees. She's wearing a black dress that hugs her hips. It has short sleeves that display her arms and give off a prim vibe while somehow remaining unbelievably sexy, and the scooped neckline that demurely covers her cleavage nearly pushes me over the edge.

I *want* her.

Now.

I move toward her, and she turns her head at the last moment and sees me, color rushing to her cheeks. She hasn't forgotten that day, either.

"Vivienne."

She tightens her grip on her purse. "Mr. Wilder."

I grin at her, and her answering smile takes my breath away. "You can call me Dominic."

She looks at me with wide eyes. "Are you sure that's a good idea? You are, after all, my boss's boss's boss."

"I've had worse ideas." I let the sentence hang in the air and she bites her lip again, and I know, right then, that we're tumbling over into uncharted territory.

"Like what?"

I lean in, like I'm about to whisper a secret into her ear. "Nothing we should be discussing at work."

Vivienne flushes a deeper red. "I'm more than ready to leave." The suggestion is there in her voice, and I want to sweep her off her feet right then.

"Me, too." I offer her my arm, and she slips her hand in, that same heat rushing through me the instant she's touching me. My heart pounds in my chest. This is fucking risky. I'm the owner of the company—I can do whatever I damn well please—but if somebody twists this the wrong way—

Then fuck them.

We move toward the entrance. "What kept you here so late?"

"I was coordinating the Mumbai meeting, and I had to be on the call."

"How did it go?"

"Fine."

She's trembling, just slightly, though her voice never wavers. We go through the front doors, and there's my car, waiting by the curb. I step up and open the door, and Vivienne slides into the backseat. I get in beside her and pull the door closed behind me.

"We're not at work anymore."

Her eyes are bright, even in the dark interior of the car. "What does that mean…Dominic?" My name in her mouth makes me want to hear her moan it with pleasure, and my cock jumps at the thought.

"We can talk about anything we want now."

Her breasts rise and fall under her dress as she breathes. "What do you want to talk about?"

"You." Her eyes lock on mine, and her lips part. "I've thought of you every day. You've been on my mind constantly." She's breathing harder now. "Can you blame me?"

Her next word is a whisper so sensual I almost lean across and crush my mouth against hers. "No."

CHAPTER NINE

Vivienne

THE AIR CRACKLES BETWEEN US. I WANT NOTHING MORE IN the world than to lean across and run my fingers over Dominic's neat stubble, feel the roughness under my fingertips, and then kiss him, finally getting to taste a man who's been haunting my dreams for three weeks.

I want it *so* badly.

But all the rationalization in the world can't work around the problem that I'm the undercover FBI agent investigating his company. Getting close to him—that I could explain. But sleeping with him could ruin me, if it ever got out, and there's no guarantee it would stay a secret.

Up close, in the back of his car, gliding through the streets of New York City, it's getting harder and harder to care. He smells like expensive soap and a hint of spicy cologne, and the shadows in the back seat play over his jawline like a damn symphony. There's not enough air in here to get a full breath, and now that he's dropped all the professional demeanor from the office, I can hardly get a handle on the way he's looking at me with a cold laser focus that's burning up underneath. We've gone three blocks, and my panties are already damp.

No, I can't blame him. I can't blame him at all, because I've thought of him every day, too. The scrape on my knee has healed, but part of me wishes it was still bleeding because then I could ask for his help. It's a pathetic impulse, but I want his hands on me so badly I'm willing to make any excuse.

"Did you think I forgot about you, Vivienne Davis?"

His next question goes straight to my chest, and it's a struggle to keep my face from betraying my relief. "Of course," I say, and my light tone almost sounds genuine. "Women probably drop doughnuts in front of you every day."

He doesn't follow my lead, doesn't joke. "They don't," he says simply. "But that's not why I've been thinking about you."

A chill runs from the top of my head to the small of my back. Maybe I'm mistaking this entirely. Maybe he knows who I am, what I'm doing, and this is his way of telling me. "Why have you been thinking of me?"

His gaze on me is hard, piercing, like he's looking right into my soul. "Because you captivated me. Because you didn't get starstruck. Something about the way you spoke, the way you moved—" He shakes his head, frustrated. "I can't get you out of my head. And your eyes—" He reaches out, brushing a stray tendril of hair away from my face. "I see your eyes in my dreams."

The bulge protruding in his pants tells me that these aren't dreams where we go out to dinner and walk along the boardwalk, and the heat between my legs increases. I feel like I'm falling, literally falling, into his blue eyes, and when his fingertips brush my skin, I can't hide the full-body shiver that moves through me. "I've been looking for you every day." My voice is barely above a whisper, but it's all I can manage with his face inches from mine, his hand still playing over the side of my neck, his touch feather-light on my shoulder.

"It's torture, isn't it?" His voice is low, almost a growl. "I sit in meetings every day and wonder what you're doing, down there in Executive Support."

I suck in a breath. "That's a lie, Dominic Wilder."

He runs his fingers down my arm to my wrist. "What's a lie?"

"You already know what I do all day at the office." I can't believe I'm about to say this, but the words are coming fast, and it's been a long day, and I might never get another chance to say any of this to him. "You wonder what I do all night."

His fingers close around my wrist, and my mind is flooded with the sensation of him doing the same to the other wrist, pinning my arms above my head, taking control, taking control of *me.* I gasp, and he leans in closer, then lifts my wrist from my lap and takes my hand in his, turning it palm upward.

"Does it have to do with these hands of yours?"

He traces my palm with one fingertip, his neatly maintained nail dragging across the sensitive skin. "What—what do you mean?" I want to tip my head back, want to close my eyes, want to let him do what he wants with me, but I stay focused on his face. This is already out of control, but I can't let it go completely off the rails. I can't. I *can't.*

"When you're all by yourself, alone, at night." It's not a question, but I hear what he's asking between the lines.

I swallow hard. "When I'm all alone at night—" I meet his eyes, not looking away. "And I'm alone *every* night—I think of you."

"Do you imagine me in my office?" There's a low note of humor in his voice that's lost in his touch as he circles my palm with his fingertip again.

"No."

"Where do you imagine me?"

"In—in a bedroom." I don't know who I am anymore, don't know why I'm giving him honest answers when honesty with this man could mean the end of my career. I squeeze my thighs together on the seat, willing myself to keep them closed, keep them *closed*, despite the urge to spread them for him, to climb onto his lap, to—

"With you?"

He leans down and presses his lips to my hand, and I can't stop myself from gasping. "Yes. With me."

"I'd love to be in a bedroom with you." He lifts his head, eyes burning into mine, and I see that he's being just as honest, just as raw, and I'm drowning in it, drowning in my want for him, and I can't do it, I have to swim. I have to tread water. Because if this goes on for much longer, I know what it's going to turn into, and I'm not going to be able to say no.

"I didn't tell you my address," I blurt out, and Dominic frowns. It's that same frown that he gave me when he first saw me on the sidewalk, like he couldn't quite figure out what I was doing and he didn't like it.

"Your address?" He lowers my hand back into my lap, and some of the air floods back into the car.

"To—to give me a ride home." I twist away from him, against the will of every cell in my body, and look out the window. "Oh, we're—we're actually right near my building. It's just a half a block up."

"Pull over." The clipped command to the driver makes my heart sink. The car glides over to the curb at the next opening, and I turn back to face Dominic.

"Is this close enough, Ms. Davis?"

He's already pulling back, pulling away from me, his body retreating, and I hate it. *Hate* it.

"Yes." I force a smile onto my face. "Thank you so much for... for the ride."

I get out of the car and take a big gulp of the summer air. His car pulls away, disappearing into the traffic, and I stumble across the sidewalk, lean my back against the building.

I should be relieved.

Instead, I'm heartbroken.

CHAPTER TEN

Dominic

THAT WAS A FUCKING DISASTER.

Or it was a disaster narrowly avoided.

I can't decide which.

I don't want to decide which.

I go back to my penthouse on the Upper East Side and pour myself a drink, then abandon it on the kitchen counter.

What the fuck is happening between me and Vivienne Davis? One minute she's fire, and the next she's ice. It doesn't make any goddamn sense.

I thunder into my bedroom. *I'd love to be in a bedroom with you.* What about that statement made her suddenly remember that she was there for a ride home and nothing else? And why am I so pissed about it? Most women never have a chance to get cold feet about doing anything with me, but the few who have gotten the privilege would never dream of it.

I can't bang open the dresser drawer in my walk-in closet, because it opens automatically at my touch, which leeches a little bit of the rage out of my chest. I don't even know why I'm so angry. I'm flirting with failure because this woman is taking all of my attention, and I have bigger things to worry about—namely, the FBI investigation trying to catch someone who's stealing information from my company to give to the Chinese government. Or someone worse than the Chinese government. Either way, I can't fathom who it would be, can't fathom how this is going to play out.

I'll keep my word to Chris. I'll sit on this for another few weeks. But it makes me furious, this waiting game.

But the way Vivienne turned on a dime—it renders me perfectly fucking helpless. Like when I watched my father destroy his own business by investing more of himself in vacations and hobbies. Like when my mother destroyed herself because she couldn't bear the loss.

Fuck feeling helpless.

Why did I open the dresser drawer in the first place? I peer down into it, finally registering that it's a drawer with neatly folded workout clothes, all in a row—socks, shorts, custom tanks that are tailored to fit me and made from a cutting-edge fabric that was just released last year. This is what I have to enjoy instead of Vivienne, and it all pales in comparison.

I snatch an outfit out of the drawer anyway and strip off the clothes I wore to the office, throwing them into a hamper built into another section of the closet.

Five minutes later, I'm running on the treadmill in my exercise room, appointed with top-of-the-line equipment, staring out at the lights of Manhattan and not seeing any of them, as I crank the speed up increment by increment until my lungs are screaming and my legs are burning, and still, all I can think of is Vivienne and wondering what it was that made her run from me.

If I was willing to take the risk, why wasn't she?

* * *

I run until I can barely draw in a breath, then go to the free weights, running through an old routine until my muscles are screaming at me to stop.

It's still not enough to wipe her from my mind.

If anything, she's taking up more real estate there because of what happened tonight.

Forget her.

I ignore my own order.

Forget her now.

I ignore it harder.

She'll destroy you.

It's bullshit, and I know it. She wants to be mine. I can see it in her eyes until the very moment I can't see it anymore, and then I don't know what the hell I'm seeing.

I put the weights back on the rack and head to the shower.

It's well after eleven by the time I get out from under the steaming water, skin sensitive from the heat, and pull on clean boxers and a t-shirt. My sheets are the highest thread count available on the market, and I slide between them, relishing the smoothness against my aching limbs.

It's a long time before I fall asleep.

* * *

At five in the morning, I give up.

I can't stop thinking about her, and no amount of exercise is going to cure that, so I order breakfast to be sent to my room and start checking today's news. I make it until six-thirty before I head into the office. I might as well get a head start on whatever paperwork I need to wade through. I can lose myself in contract details until...

Until the day ends, and then I'll have to figure out something else to do, lest I lose my damn mind.

I'm so distracted that I get into the regular elevator and let myself off on the ninth floor instead of going to my office. I don't know what the hell I think there is for me on the ninth floor—most of it is still in semi-darkness, the morning light not yet filtering in through the windows at full strength.

I'm about to turn around and get back into the elevator when movement in one of the offices catches my eye.

The bank of executive offices runs along the back of the floor, but the movement is coming from the opposite end, near one of the cubicles. Whoever it is leans awkwardly over the station, clicking through something. His movements are hesitant, like he's not quite sure what he's looking at. Something about this doesn't seem right. Most of the people at this level don't come in until 9 a.m., a perk I've allowed for several years.

When he straightens up, I see that it's not one of the executives, it's someone from the staff. Probably one of the people on the tech team. He pulls his phone from his pocket, swipes across, and then scurries off to one of the other offices. Undoubtedly tech support. Those guys work strange hours, coming in early to make adjustments to the system.

I get back into the elevator and go up to my office.

The day stretches out ahead of me, endless and empty. The office is quiet—even Emily doesn't arrive until seven forty-five most days—and though the scene outside my window is bathed in early summer light, it doesn't make an impression.

She's still all I can think of.

CHAPTER ELEVEN

Vivienne

I WAKE UP EARLY IN THE MORNING, AFTER A NIGHT SPENT tossing and turning beneath my sheets. They're a tangled mess, and so is my mind.

I don't know what I was thinking getting into that car with Dominic last night.

I shouldn't have agreed to a ride home—I shouldn't have answered the call. It was ten o'clock at night, I'd been at the office all day, and it's so damn unprofessional.

But I *wanted* him.

I wanted him so much that it kept me up most of the rest of the night, and when I dozed off a few hours ago, I fell into fitful dreams of him. Most of them were unbearably sexy, but at some point, every time, his eyes would go cold and distant, and

I'd know that I'd said the wrong thing, done the wrong thing, and that it was over.

I throw myself onto my back and cover my eyes with my hands with a groan. Morning light is filtering around the edges of my curtains, but I'm exhausted.

And horny.

And sorry.

I'm wishing I could explain myself to him. I'm wishing any part of this was normal, was *real*, so that I could just tell him everything and ask him out on a date.

I laugh, and it sounds bitter even to me. For some reason, Dominic let me see that he wanted me last night, but does he want to *date* me? I'm not billionaire material. Well, I *am* billionaire material—I'm not about to start devaluing myself—but I'm a career girl. I want to climb the ranks and do well for myself. I'm not about to spend the rest of my days hanging off some man's arm like a decoration.

Even that thought doesn't ring true, but the words in my mind are becoming jumbled, completely overtaken by the pulsing throb between my legs.

I still want Dominic Wilder, and now that I've had the chance and ruined it for myself, I want him even more.

I get out of bed, frustrated as hell, and stomp over to my dresser. There, in the top drawer, covered neatly with a layer of my going-out panties—most of those haven't seen the light of day since I joined the FBI—is a sleek black vibrator, top of the line. I bought it for myself a few years ago, thinking it would make some of the lonely nights easier. Before Dominic, the lonely nights were seeming like a small problem.

I hate that he has this effect on me.

But I can't deny it, not now, not this morning. The urge is too strong.

I slip off my t-shirt and panties and slide back under the sheets, laying against the pillow with a sigh, and close my eyes.

This time, I don't fight it.

I let myself linger on those deep blue eyes of his, on his low voice whispering dirty things into my ear, of his hands, so powerful yet so gentle, caressing my skin. I want to know what he would look like stripping off his clothes, coming to me with his cock already hard and ready. And me—

Me, on the bed, on my hands and knees, ass pressed up into the air, exposed and open for him, waiting.

I flip the switch on the vibrator and bring its silicon surface to my pussy. I'm already wet, and I trace over my folds and bite my lip.

Me, on the bed, spread open wide, waiting, nipples hard even before he starts to trace his tongue around them, teasing me, torturing me, bringing me closer and closer to the edge of sheer, blinding pleasure.

Me, bent over his desk, skirt shoved up around my waist, one of his hands evoking a gentle pressure there, one thundering down onto the bare flesh of my ass, the heat and pain turning me on.

I gasp in the silence of my apartment. This is the part of me that's filthy, that's not professional, that's not strong and independent, not like I am in the daylight, at my job, in the world. This is the part of me that feels the uncertainty of the earth beneath my feet and wants badly just to have someone else take the reins for a while. The part of me that gets a dirty thrill to think of a man spanking me, punishing me, and how much I might enjoy it.

I press the vibrator harder against my clit, circling it again and again. I imagine the punishment, the spanking, turning into pleasure, turning into this, the reward settling in while my ass still stings, and then Dominic thrusting into me from behind, taking me, filling me, his thighs pressing again and again into my punished bottom, the pain and the pleasure mixing into a sweet high that I ride over and over until I can't come again, until he comes hard into me, and then I explode over the vibrator, my hips jerking away from the surface of the bed, rising with each wave until there are no more waves to ride.

I turn the vibrator off and toss it to the floor, feeling the heat in my face, feeling the blush rising to my cheeks. These are secret fantasies, the kind Dominic can never know. The kind nobody can ever know.

I roll over. It's still two hours before my alarm is set to go off, before I have to get into the shower and get dressed and walk into Wilder Industries like nothing happened last night, like everything is fine. Now that I've come by thinking of him—and not for the first time—I can sense sleep settling down over me like a blanket, relaxing my muscles, carrying me away.

I'm almost there, almost slipping into a peaceful dream, when the thought occurs to me, crystal clear and plain as day.

I can't leave things like this.

What happened last night might not have been *wrong*, but I don't like how we—I—left things. I don't like how coldness crept into the moment, how Dominic turned away from me.

It might not be professional. It might not be right. But I owe him an apology, and I'm going to give it to him.

Just as soon as I wake up.

CHAPTER TWELVE

Dominic

I TEAR THROUGH THE MORNING'S PAPERWORK AND LEAD THE meetings with more enthusiasm than usual. I want to get things done. I am sick of letting Vivienne Davis control my thoughts, and so I refuse to let her.

Much.

At ten o'clock, all the paperwork for the day is done, and we're ahead of schedule on status meetings. Most of the afternoon is free. I can change that.

But first, I'm going to go for a walk. There's a café at the end of the block that makes delicious iced coffee and I've never been able to get anyone at the Wilder Building to duplicate it. It's so relentlessly beautiful outside my window that I can't resist. Now that I'm back on track, it's fine to indulge for a few minutes.

I go out past Emily's desk, and she looks up at me when I stop in front of it. "Mr. Wilder," she says with a smile. "You're ahead of schedule today."

"Thanks to you." Her cheeks go a little pink. Emily is unwaveringly professional, but sometimes she can't quite control her reactions when I've done something to please her. "Is there anything on Monday that we could move up? I have a gap in my schedule."

She swivels her chair toward her computer screen and deftly navigates to next week's calendar. "I'm not exactly sure. I can make a few contacts and follow up with you. Will you be gone long?"

"I'm just walking to the café."

She nods at me and smiles again. "I'll have a list of options for you to review when you get back."

Since I've come out this way, I decide to take the public elevator down to the lobby. If I can move some of those meetings to this afternoon, it could free up time Monday morning to explore some of the options I've been meaning to get more intel on in terms of new energy patents we might want to acquire before they get too far into the process. This is an area in which my father unquestionably failed. He didn't go after new tech aggressively enough. He didn't go after *anything* aggressively enough, but his distractions were the things that undid him in the end.

The elevator stops, and I look up at the floor indicator, forgetting for a second that I'm not in my private car.

The doors slide open.

And in steps Vivienne Davis.

She's looking down at the contents of a folder in her hands and gives me a cursory glance for just long enough to step out of my way, and then she does a double take and blushes a deep red.

"Oh, I—" She turns automatically toward the doors, but they're already sliding shut. To her credit, she doesn't try to pretend that she was about to bolt. She squares her shoulders and turns to face me. "Mr. Wilder."

"Ms. Davis."

It's there already, sizzling between us while we stand together in this relatively confined space. It's hard to look into her eyes, but I'll be damned if I'm going to let her see that she kept me up half the night.

One corner of her mouth turns up. "You can call me Vivienne."

The sound of her voice, softening like that, makes my chest go tight, and I can't keep up the pretense. "I don't know, Ms. Davis. We've been through this before, and it didn't turn out very well."

She bites her lip. "I know. I was hoping—" The elevator starts moving downward, and she steps farther in and turns to face the doors. We're shoulder to shoulder for a moment, and then she turns to face me, green eyes locked on mine. "I was hoping to run into you."

The sentence comes out in a rush, like she's been holding it in for a long time. Maybe she has.

"What for?"

I can't look away from her. I don't want to look away from her.

"I wanted to apologize."

"You don't owe me an apology, Ms. Davis."

She flinches, just a little, but I see it. "Please," she says quietly, and there's something there in her voice, something open and honest. "Call me Vivienne."

"Vivienne, you don't have to do anything that makes you uncomfortable. Clearly, something I did last night made you uncomfortable." I clear my throat, not dropping her gaze. "And it was wrong. It was inappropriate, unprofessional, and—"

"It wasn't wrong." She breaks in so suddenly that I'm taken aback. Her cheeks are still pink, flushed, and she's clutching the folder to her chest. "It's not wrong to—feel attracted to someone." Her eyes are on the floor indicator, which is ticking steadily down to the lobby. "I'm sorry I reacted that way. Something you said—it just reminded me that I'm supposed to be professional, I *work* for you, and—"

"And it doesn't matter, does it?" It's her turn to look a little shocked, and I step closer. She takes a single step back and hits the wall, her back pressed against the shining surface. "It doesn't matter, because even though it's not appropriate, you still can't stop thinking about me."

"I can't," she whispers.

"Do you know how I know?"

"How?"

My face is inches from hers. I breathe in the light scent of her perfume. "I can't stop thinking about you, either. I'm not supposed to have you, Vivienne Davis, but I want you." Her breath is shallow, fast. "I wasn't lying when I said it last night, and I'm not lying now. I want you, and I don't give a shit that you work three levels below me."

"Two," she blurts out. She's caught between a smile and a frown.

"What?"

"Two levels below you," she says, nodding down at the folder. "I did such a wonderful job on the Mumbai meeting that I got promoted. I'm going to be Mr. Overhiser's chief executive assistant."

Closer and closer and closer. Somehow, she's getting closer to me with every day. Chief executive assistants attend meetings in place of executives when they're double booked. They coordinate with Emily to make sure any individual meetings work with my schedule.

I don't want to fire her.

I don't want to derail her career.

And I can't let her go.

It's in this moment, right now, that I make up my mind.

"Two levels. Is that all?"

"Yes," she says, her voice dropping as I lean in closer, my lips just next to her ear.

"Somehow that makes it more inappropriate, don't you think?"

She can't speak. She only nods.

"I have a solution."

Her eyes go wide and bright, and she's holding very still, like it's all she can do not to turn her head and kiss me right now. "What is it?"

"I want to spend time with you, Vivienne Davis. I want to spend time with you alone. I want to spend time with you in places where we can talk about anything, because I have to know more about you."

"But how—"

"I'll keep a secret," I whisper, and then I lean in and take her earlobe between my teeth so gently that it won't leave the hint of a mark. She gasps, hands going tight around the folder in her hands. "We'll keep it a secret, and nobody has to know."

"*Yes.*" She breathes the word and a jolt of satisfaction fills me, warms me, threatens to burn me up.

I step away from her. There's an instant of confusion on her face, and then the elevator *dings,* and the doors slide open.

I turn and move to step out, to act like nothing has happened. It's all part of the game now.

"Yes," she says after me, her voice clear and strong. "Yes."

CHAPTER THIRTEEN

Vivienne

T HE WEEKEND IS AGONY, A BLUR OF THINKING, OVER AND over again, *what the hell am I doing?*

There are a million reasons not to go near Dominic Wilder. This *job,* for one. My entire *career,* for two. And beyond all that— beyond the humiliation I would likely suffer if anyone breathes a word of this to my boss—there's the fact that Dominic and I live in different worlds. He's like some of the guys I dated in college— rich and arrogant. Clearly, if what transpired in the elevator is any indication, he'll pursue what he wants.

No. He's different.

The argument brewing in the back of my mind is a quiet one, but part of me wants to believe it's true. After that horribly disap- pointing ride back to my apartment the other night, it's not like he had any regrets and decided to get out of the car and follow me upstairs to make it right, demanding what he wanted from me.

What we *both* wanted.

Still...

I fill the weekend with as much activity as I can. I run for miles in the mornings around Central Park, coming home with sweat beading on my skin, my tired legs cramping and achy, and my mind still wrapped up in sultry thoughts of Dominic no matter how loudly I blare the music from my iPhone hoping to drown out the vivid images. I always play music while I run, even though I know better than to block out my surroundings like that, but today I turn it *up.*

I know better than to feel giddy about getting a secret shot at hooking up with Dominic Wilder. I know so much better than that, but I can't help myself.

He doesn't call or text over the weekend, so I go back and forth puzzling to myself about what this means like I'm a love-struck high schooler. He *has* to have my cell number...or maybe he doesn't. He could probably look it up any time he wants since I'm sure he has access to my personnel file, and it *is* the work mobile the company assigned to me. I spent hours memorizing the number, and I never carry my real phone with me—just in case. But it never rings, never buzzes with an alert from him or anyone else. Over the weekend, my real phone hums with alerts seemingly non-stop. My best friend, Margo, knows something is up when I ask if she wants to go to a museum on Saturday afternoon.

"Which museum?" Her voice sounds skeptical over the phone.

"I don't know, the MoMA? Maybe a different one?"

"You *never* want to go to a museum."

"I want to today."

"Are you going to tell me what's got you all riled up?"

"No."

It's not that I don't want to spill my guts to Margo, but she's not FBI, and I'm already pushing the boundaries with this job too far.

She sighs. "Fine. But I don't want to look at art forever. Let's get sushi afterward."

"Deal."

She spends the entire time we're touring the museum—none of the art seems to be making any kind of impression on her—giving me the side-eye and trying to guess what it is that's made me so desperate that I'd go as far as planning a cultural afternoon in New York City.

"Did you get fired?"

Not yet. "No, I'm still gainfully employed."

"Did you...meet a guy?"

Yes, but I can't tell you about him, and I'll probably never be able to tell you about him, because after this... "I meet guys at work every day, but no, that's not it." The lie tastes sour on my tongue, but I can't let this discussion build any further.

When Sunday night comes, I lie awake for hours, flipping and flopping in my bed, wondering if I imagined everything that happened between us in the elevator, wondering if all this tossing and turning is only meant to distract me from something that never happened at all.

***

The white envelope is sitting on my desk when I arrive to work on Monday morning at eight forty-five. It's early enough to make a good impression, yet late enough to let anyone who might be the least bit curious know that I'm *not* desperate to get back to the Wilder Enterprises offices, like I didn't masturbate at least twice a day with my vibrator, like the heat between my legs doesn't increase with every step I take toward the imposing skyscraper, all because of Dominic Wilder.

It looks like a normal envelope at first glance, but the moment I touch it, I know it's from *him.* It's of even higher quality than the high-end office supplies used at Wilder Enterprises.

I anxiously glance back over my shoulder, once, twice. Marie isn't here yet, or else she'd have poked her head around the cubicle wall and demanded to know what I did all weekend. Ms. Lillianfield is *probably* here—she's never late, always too early—but she makes it a habit not to start her rounds until 9 a.m. The woman might be terse, but she's fair. I can pretty much guarantee that she's not involved with any in-house espionage.

Focus on that, I tell myself. *That's your real job.* Then I sit down and tear open the envelope.

Something shiny and silver falls out of the envelope into my lap, and I pick it up before I even have a chance to read the words on the notepaper tucked inside. It's a delicate necklace, and after another moment I don't think it's silver after all. I think it's platinum, or something even nicer. Hanging from the fragile chain is a teardrop diamond.

A sunbeam shining in through the window catches the diamond and casts a rainbow over my desk, and I gasp at the delight that floods my chest.

It *was* real, then. This necklace is expensive—too expensive for anyone I know to have bought it—but discreet enough that I can wear it in the office and not draw too much attention.

I look down at the note.

V—

I didn't want to invade your privacy for your cell phone number, but rest assured that I thought of you all weekend. I'd like to see you wearing this as your only accessory. Wear it for me today and meet me at Rouge at nine o'clock tonight. A car will pick you up at your place at eight forty-five.

—D

The Vivienne Davis who's spent the last few years clawing her way up the ranks at the FBI would never fall for this, but maybe I'm not that Vivienne Davis, because my hands tremble with excitement as I put the necklace around my neck and hook the clasp. Rouge is a new high-end French restaurant that's impossible to get into, and all I can think about is what I'm going to wear. There's no doubt in my mind that I'm going.

I hear footsteps heading down the row of cubicles toward my desk, and before anyone can discover what I'm doing I tuck the note back in the envelope and slip it into one of my desk drawers. I'm just sliding it shut when a bright, beaming face framed by bouncy red curls bursts around the corner into my work space.

"Viv!" She cries my name like we haven't seen each other in a hundred years. "What did you do all weekend? I had dates with two different men—I know, I'm taking such a big *risk.* I'm living on the edge. What about you?"

"Well, I—" *I spent all weekend fantasizing about pursuing a secret relationship with Dominic Wilder.*

Marie doesn't wait for me to respond. She drops into her chair and rolls backward so she can look over at me again. "Hey, nice necklace!"

CHAPTER FOURTEEN

Dominic

The Vivienne standing in the entrance to the Rouge's dining room is a damn vision in red, the satiny fabric of her dress hugging every one of her luscious curves. I want to be that dress. No—I want to take that dress off of her, slide my hands along every divine inch of her creamy, soft skin until I find every single one of the places that make those pretty lips part, that make her gasp and tremble and never want to pull away from me.

But I have to be patient. There will be time for all that.

That's what I keep telling myself—we have time. My heart races at the sight of her, trying to will my mind into rushing through this evening, but I won't. She has her reasons to be skittish, I'm sure.

Tonight I'm going to do my damnedest to find out what they are.

She hesitates just a moment longer, and a tuxedoed waiter glides to her side. I see her mouth my name, and the words on her lips make me hard all over again.

Patience.

The waiter guides her through the elegant tables, each adorned with a spotless heavy white linen tablecloth, each with two or four people seated around its edges, all beaming at their incredible luck at getting a reservation at one of New York's hottest new places.

I didn't need luck.

All I had to do was say my name and the management found a table for me. Not just any table, either, but a quiet table for two hidden in a private alcove with a window overlooking the river.

If Vivienne's reservations are similar to my worries—that her reputation might be smeared by being out in public on what's clearly a date with a man who is essentially her boss—then this alcove should put her mind at ease. She couldn't see it from the door of the dining room. I didn't notice it myself at first, which tells me we're safely hidden away here.

Just to be extra cautious, I've slipped the members of the wait staff assigned to our table a hefty tip, and we haven't even started our evening yet.

The waiter shows Vivienne to the table and swiftly disappears as soon as she thanks him. Then her green eyes are fixed on my face, and a blush rises to her cheeks.

"Wow. You pulled out all the stops, Mr. Wilder."

"Dominic," I correct her automatically, standing up and stepping over to her. "And this is *hardly* all the stops."

The air hums with her anticipation. I move in closer, my hand lightly touching her elbow, and lean down to kiss her cheek. My reward is the hint of a gasp, a quick intake of breath that tells me she's as much on edge as I am, just as ready to be here with me as I am to be here with her.

But that's as far as I take it, and her shoulders slink back down into place as I pull out her chair and slide it back underneath her as she takes her seat. She tucks her little purse down next to her chair and then straightens her back in her seat, beaming across at me with a sweet smile as I take my place across from her.

"I take it you like the necklace?"

The single diamond gleams just above her breasts, framed perfectly by the neckline of her dress, and her cheeks go a little pinker and her eyes twinkle. "It's gorgeous." She leans in a little closer. "And discreet."

"I thought about it carefully—too much of a statement piece would have drawn a bit too much attention, don't you think?"

She considers me again, her eyes dancing in the candlelight. "You're different."

"Different how?"

"Different...*now*."

I know what she means. Being in this restaurant with me, at

least for the moment, seems to have tempered Vivienne's snappy attitude, softened her edges a bit. The energy she's radiating tonight is more sensual than nervous.

It makes me want her more with every second that passes.

"It's different, outside of the office."

"Tell me about it."

She looks down onto the finely printed menu, smiling to herself, and we're off.

Over a glass of the restaurant's best Cabernet Sauvignon, I ask her the first question that's been bothering me since I saw her on the sidewalk. "Have you lived in New York all your life?"

She gives me a coy look. "Do I sound like a native New Yorker?"

"Not at all."

"I grew up in Michigan."

"Why'd you leave?"

She shrugs a little, cuts her eyes to the side, the stem of her wine glass held lightly in her right hand. "I wanted bigger things than a small farming town could offer."

"Bigger things...like the Executive Support Department at Wilder Enterprises?" She seems too smart, too poised, for that to be her greatest aspiration.

Vivienne grins at me, but there's a hint of something in her eyes that I can't quite place. "I'm planning to work my way up."

"That's the right attitude to have." I don't want to talk about work, I don't want to talk about the office, and I'm betting she doesn't really, either. "Do your parents miss you now that you live so far away?"

She laughs a little. "Oh, I'm sure they do. But they wanted each of us to be independent, not clingers."

"Us?"

"I have a sister, Delilah."

"Older or younger?"

"Younger, by two years." She sips at her wine and places the glass back down on the table. "Do you really want to know about my sister and parents?"

The honest answer comes before I can stop it. "No, I want to talk about you." The grin on her face turns a little bit wicked. "What makes you so irresistible?"

"I could ask you the same question."

"That's an easy answer." I lean in like it's a state secret. "It's my fabulous wealth."

Vivienne cocks her head to the side. "That *is* a plus." She lets her phrase linger in the air for a moment. "But that's not all of it."

"My good looks, of course."

"You're very modest."

"I don't know that modesty is always a virtue."

She blushes at that. "No? When is it not a virtue?"

"In elevators, for instance. Or in cars." The charge in the air kicks up another notch, and the waiter arrives at that moment to deliver the main course. I hardly notice. Vivienne doesn't even pause to glance down at her plate.

"You're not being very fair."

"How am I not being fair? You love this restaurant."

Her eyes sparkling, she nods. "It's gorgeous. Lovely."

"Like you."

She shakes her head shyly. "But when you talk about those places..."

"Does your mind get overtaken by certain...memories?"

"Certain memories...and certain sensations."

"Sensations that you'd like to experience again?"

She bites her lip, glancing down at her plate for the first time, then looking back up into my eyes. "I shouldn't want to." Her voice drops to almost a whisper.

"You're free to want anything in the world, even if other people think otherwise." I reach my hand across the table and take hers in mine, the electricity sparking back and forth between us. "And do you know what, Vivienne Davis?"

"What?"

"I'm free to give it to you."

I hold her gaze for another long moment, watching her imagine all the things we could do together, and then I put her hand back down. She sucks in a breath.

"But I think," I say, keeping my tone languid, "that we should start...with..."

"With leaving?"

"With dinner."

She laughs, and my heart sings.

CHAPTER FIFTEEN

Vivienne

THE RESTAURANT IS FABULOUS, AND EVERY SINGLE BITE OF the food—French entrées I hardly recognize the names of but can't stop eating until they're gone—explodes on my tongue. Part of me can't believe I'm here, eating this fancy, expensive meal, with a man like Dominic, and that's the part that wants to stare at the elegant, understated decor and run my hands down the tablecloth, which I'm almost convinced has a higher thread count than my sheets.

But most of me is consumed with Dominic.

He seems at ease in the restaurant, ordering different wines, anticipating the exact moment the waiter will be back, tearing a roll in two and dipping it delicately into a delicately flavorful sauce I've never tasted before. Once I sample it, I want to keep eating it for the rest of the night.

More than that, I want to keep drinking Dominic in.

Away from the overhead lighting of the Wilder Building—which is high-end overhead lighting, for *sure*—he seems like more of the high-powered billionaire, yet less like him at the same time. Clearly, though, he's in his element here. He never hesitates to make a choice, or order more of something if he sees that I'm enjoying it. He's in absolute control, and it's making me even more crazy for him. If he's this comfortable casually dominating the wait staff, what will he be like behind closed doors?

With me?

On the other hand, he's calm in a way that I haven't seen at Wilder Enterprises. Whenever I've watched him there, he's always on edge, the air around him crackling with tension, the type of tension that doesn't seem like it's the result of being attracted to another person so much as it's about something happening behind the scenes, under the surface, where I can't see it.

By the time the waiter whisks away the last of the plates, I'm somehow in absolute heaven, full but not overstuffed, already daydreaming of the next time I'll get to eat something this delicious.

Dominic offers me his hand, and the daydream comes to an abrupt end, but in favor of a new dream that's starting up right in front of me.

"Thank you so much," I say as he tucks my hand into his arm, not bothering to make a production out of it. This place must really be a kind of safe haven if he's not worrying about anyone seeing us so closely knit to one another.

Or, says a snotty little voice in the back of my mind, *he doesn't care if anyone sees us here. You're a nobody. You could be anybody. Maybe he just knows that no one who could impact his work, his life, could ever afford to come here.*

I shove those thoughts out my mind and let him escort me out of the restaurant. I keep my eyes focused straight ahead, occasionally letting them travel over the line of his jaw, noticing the way his collar is tailored so perfectly that only a single fingertip could fit between the fabric and his shoulders. Out of the corner of my eye, I can see patrons' heads turning toward us, watching us, but I must be imagining the whispers.

Dominic doesn't seem to care at all. His strides are even and powerful, and it feels like I'm floating along atop the carpet, until we reach the front doors—held open by two more uniformed waiters—and exit into the car waiting for us at the curb.

This isn't the black Town Car he took me home in last week. This is something on another level, something sleek, fast-looking and curvy, a deep wine color that's only a few shades lighter than black. I'm not half bad at recognizing cars, but what with the amount of wine I drank, and the amazingly delicious and filling food, and being so close to Dominic—intoxicating in itself—I can't place the model.

It's not until he's sitting next to me in the back seat, the engine purring as the driver pulls away from the curb, that I find the words to ask. "What kind of car is this?"

"Do you really want to talk about cars?" His eyes are glittering in the sultry darkness of the backseat.

"No."

He leans in, his warm breath tickling my earlobe, sending shivers of pleasure down my spine. "It's an Audi—so new they haven't even introduced it to the public yet."

I breathe him in as he slides over, eliminating the space between us, wrapping one arm around my shoulders and sliding it down until it's around my waist, pulling me closer into his body. "If it's not for sale yet—" I'm somehow short of breath already. "Does that mean you always get what you want?"

"Vivienne Davis, you should already know that I *always* get what I want."

"What—" I suck in one more breath. "What do you want now?" I know what *I* want, and it's turning me into a mindless puddle.

His lips hover near my ear one more time. "You."

I turn my head and, not being able to hold back any longer, crush my lips against his. I can't wait another moment and so I don't. I just kiss him, hard and hot, relishing his arm tightening around me. He twists, pressing me back into the buttery-soft luxury leather seat, and as his tongue pushes into my mouth, his other hand is playing at my knee. He doesn't ask, doesn't insist, but

I spread my legs wider on instinct, wanting him to have access, wanting him to touch me, to *please* touch me.

He bites my lip so gently that I moan into his mouth. The professional Vivienne Davis, undercover FBI agent, is gone, and I'm just a woman, a bundle of live nerves spread out on a billionaire's back seat, his strong hand stroking the bare skin there, his tongue exploring my mouth, and then his lips tracing a hot path of fire down the side of my neck.

I'm soaking wet. There's no denying it, and for a fleeting instant, I worry about the car's upholstery. But that moment is over almost before it begins.

"I want you," Dominic says, his voice low, nearly a growl. "Are you going to run away again?"

"I was just—" I'm gasping for breath as his hand moves higher and higher up my leg toward my folds. "I was afraid...my job—your job—I'm—*please*, take me. *Please*, Dominic, claim me, have me, punish me." The last phrase slips out before I can stop it, and I'm in so deep that I hardly have time to be embarrassed. His hand has reached the lace panties and he hooks a finger in the waistband near my hips. I know I'm practically incoherent by this point, but I want him to touch me so badly that I can't get the words out of my mouth in order. Hell, I don't *care* about getting them in order.

He presses his lips against mine again, his finger moving slowly toward the front of my panties, toward my molten hot core, and I open my lips for him again. I don't care that we're in the back of the car, that there's a driver, I'm *so* ready for this—

Dominic pulls away, first his lips, then his hands, and I let out a groan, reaching for his shirt. I'll do this myself… I'll loosen the tie from around his neck, I'll unbutton every button.

The car is slowing and Dominic reaches up and catches my wrists in his hands, kissing me one more time.

"I'll have you, Vivienne Davis," he growls into my ear. "I'll take you like you've never been taken before."

The car is stopping at the curb, and, dazed, I realize we're in front of my apartment building.

Dominic gives me a wicked smile. "Just not quite yet."

CHAPTER SIXTEEN

Dominic

O F COURSE I WANT TO TAKE HER TO MY PENTHOUSE AND fuck her until she's senseless with pleasure. Of course I forced myself not to react when she begged me to punish her— but it was those words that told me we're on another level.

Vivienne Davis can't resist me, and my hands on her body unlock something within her I can guarantee she hasn't surrendered to anyone else. That was one of her deepest fantasies, one she would *never* admit out loud, and I heard it directly from her lips.

Deep down inside, Vivienne Davis—despite what she might say in the light of day, despite how confident and independent she is, despite everything—is desperate for someone to take control, at least in the bedroom. She needs it so badly, I can taste it in the air stirring around her. And now that I know it for sure...

It's time to play.

She's bewildered when I get out of the car and help her out, her face red and hot, her body trembling, and her breath coming fast in her throat.

"Not now?"

Her deep green eyes are wide, her lips puffy from my attention, and her face is a picture of disbelief. I lean down and kiss her cheek, just the way I did in the restaurant, then I put my hand under her arm and steer her toward the entrance to her building. "Not now."

"But—" I stop, face her, and put my finger over her mouth.

"No, no," I murmur, leaning to speak directly into her ear, feeling her body shiver underneath my touch. "Not yet, sweet thing." Another shiver. "Do you think I'm going to rush through the anticipation? No—I wouldn't do that."

She groans softly. "Dominic, I—"

"Be a good girl," I say softly into her ear. I'm taking a chance on this—for some women, it's a turnoff, but for others—

Vivienne trembles, harder than before. That's the reaction I was hoping for. She leans into me a little bit more, and I can feel the hope pulsing underneath the surface of her skin.

"Be a good girl, and I'll make it so worth it."

She opens her mouth one more time to argue, and then thinks better of it, a little frown playing over her face. I put a finger underneath her chin and lift it until she's looking directly into my eyes.

"I promise."

"Okay." The word is a whisper that's almost swallowed up in the July breeze.

"I'll see you soon."

I act like it's nothing to stop touching her, like it's nothing to walk away from her, and I don't look back.

She stands frozen on the sidewalk until the Audi disappears from sight. I lean back against the headrest and try to ignore the painful erection that's about to burst out of my pants, letting myself dissolve into the delicious anticipation that I've set in motion.

* * *

For the first time in weeks, the world seems brighter, seems suffused with a new energy, and it's all because of Vivienne. I don't see her on Tuesday morning, and still, just the knowledge that she's down on the eighth floor, walking and breathing, wearing the glittering diamond I sent to her around her neck, is putting me in a damned fantastic mood.

The one thing I didn't ask for was her phone number, and that will come with time. I'm not going to look it up—I'll wait until we're at that special point—because the fact that we have to use other means of contacting each other makes this even sexier.

Judging by the expression on her face when I drove away last night, I'm going to be on her mind—probably about as much as she's been on my mind, which is nonstop and can't even be cured by four rounds of jacking off in the shower between last night and this morning and a mind-numbing, hour-long workout at the gym.

Exchanging phone numbers comes sooner than I thought, however. Around lunch time, my private cell buzzes in my pocket, and I slide it out before I've put the next bite of steak into my mouth. The message is from an unfamiliar number, but as soon as I read the text, I know it's from her.

I wanted to call you last night, but I didn't have your number.

I can almost hear her saying it in the same low voice that she adopts when she's very, very turned on.

How did you get it this morning, sweet thing?

She'd never be able to send this from any kind of work phone, so I know it's relatively secure.

My new boss gave me a list of essentials in case of emergency...

Overhiser. He's never been one of my favorites, but he does his job well enough that firing him would be more of a hassle than it's worth. He'll age out sooner or later and retire to the Bahamas, and that will be the end of that.

This is an emergency, is it? :)

Some parts of me think so.

Which parts?

There's a long pause, and I decide to end it before she loses her nerve.

Be a good girl and tell me what has you so bothered.

Those are the magic words, and I know it's only for times like these—times when we're "alone," when we're in that sphere where the rest of the world doesn't exist. I know it instinctively. Vivienne has her sights set on a thriving career...she just has a dirty little fantasy that can play out in the secret spaces.

My pussy aches for you.

My cock is already rock-hard, but it gets impossibly harder. I adjust it in my pants and glance out the door to Emily's desk. Still empty.

Is the waiting too much for you?

No. I can handle it!

I think you're lying to me, sweet thing.

I would never lie to you.

She doesn't hesitate to send that message, which makes me think it's absolutely true.

Be patient.

It's hard.

So am I.

I want you...

I want you, Vivienne.

Have me.

Not now...

Cruel.

I'm not cruel. I'll prove it to you.

How?

There's a gift coming to your desk in the next two hours. Don't open it at the office. Take it home and follow the instructions.

The entire plan comes to me as I write out the text, a grin

spreading across my face. Then I send a second follow-up text on its heels.

Will you be a good girl?

Yes...

Tell me.

I'll be a good girl.

Get back to work and wait for your gift.

She doesn't answer.

She's gone back to work.

I click out of the text messaging app and dial a number, my heart pumping in my chest. I've got her all wound up.

She's going to love the release.

And I'm going to love imagining what she looks like as she does.

CHAPTER SEVENTEEN

Vivienne

THE WHITE BOX THAT ARRIVES ON MY DESK IS ABOUT THE SIZE of a doughnut box, and it's tied with a ribbon that walks the line between subtle discretion and understated decoration. At a glance the package looks fairly unassuming, but if I still worked in the cubicle next to Marie, she'd be all over it in less than half a second.

Even sitting alone in the reception area outside Mr. Overhiser's office, I can't convince myself that the color rising to my cheeks isn't incriminating. I only allow myself a couple of minutes to look over the box before opening the lowest drawer of my desk and depositing it carefully inside away from prying eyes.

I'm *not* supposed to open it at work. Naturally, that makes me even more anxious to open it.

Instead, I focus my attention—drag it, kicking and screaming—on my newly assigned duties.

Scheduling for Mr. Overhiser turns out to be far less complex than what I had been doing for the Executive Support team. It turns out that my main priorities include ensuring that Mr. Overhiser's favorite lunch—a specific BLT with a few finicky add-ons from the restaurant down the street—is on his desk at twelve-fifteen every day, that his meetings don't run past schedule, and that I can provide excuses if he wants to duck out for the day early.

At least that's the vibe I get in the first few hours, and my gut instincts are usually spot-on.

The entire set-up is more perfect than I could have dreamed, because while I'm making myself look busier than I really am—ordering lunch isn't rocket science, and making up excuses is simple—I'm also finally getting a crack at tackling the job I'm really here to do.

Namely, finding out if Mr. Overhiser is the inside man for the Chinese government.

I find my mind continuing to stray, though. *Do your job,* I remind myself sternly every time I start thinking about the box.

When I take my afternoon break at three o'clock, it's all I can do not to give in to temptation, to lift that simple white box out of its hiding place in the drawer, untie the ribbon, and take a *peek* inside. One look. One look can't hurt...

But he *told* me – insisted – that I not open it here, and that's the game we're playing. The game that sets my core ablaze and makes me want to play for the rest of my life.

I put a hand to my forehead and my heart jumps. That's a long time, the rest of my life—but my nerves pulse with excitement when I think about the box and what might be in it, when I think about *Dominic,* and in this moment, yeah, I'd love for this to go on for the rest of my life.

Mr. Overhiser is a Grade A creep and doesn't even pretend to hide it, but he also likes to be out of the office right at five, which is perhaps his single redeeming quality. Today, I can't wait to leave the office. The moment he steps out the office door and into the elevator, I leap from my seat, wrench open the desk drawer, and grab the box.

I'm going to have to carry it home with me—it won't quite fit in my purse, at least not well enough for it not to be awkward— and a little thrill of nervousness streaks down my spine. People sometimes snatch things from passengers on the subway. I'm not letting this baby—whatever it is—out of my grip, so that could turn into...a situation...if anyone even looks at it funny.

I walk the three blocks to the subway station as fast as I can in my three-inch black heels. The train is crowded with the rush of people heading home after work, but nobody tries to screw with me, and I'm so preoccupied about this gift that it makes the time fly. I'm breathing hard by the time I rush to my apartment. Slamming the door shut behind me, I drop my purse to the floor and carry the box to the coffee table in my living room, handling it like it's a priceless treasure.

The ribbon slips off like a dream. It would only have taken a feather-light touch to do this in the office, and it brings a smile to my face. No doubt Dominic knew that.

Now that it's time to open the box, I hesitate.

He's right—the anticipation *is* worth it. I give myself a moment—just another moment—to linger in it, imagining what I'm going to find inside. Some kind of dress I could never afford even if I saved up for it the rest of my life? An invitation to another exclusive restaurant? Will a driver be pulling up outside my building any moment to pick me up? Is Dominic waiting by his phone right now for me to call?

That's what does me in. I tear the lid off the box and look down to find something wrapped delicately in tissue paper. I toss all of it aside to reveal two objects.

One is a vibrator, but it reminds me of Dominic's car—sleek and designed within an inch of its life, probably something you can't get unless you're someone like him.

The second—I gasp out loud when I register what it is—is a butt plug.

There's no mistaking the tapered shape, the smooth silicone surface, and even though I've never seen one before, I know what it is, and there is no way I'm going to—

My heart pounds against my rib cage, and I scrape through the last few sheets of tissue paper. There's a card at the very bottom of the box, the envelope thick and heavy. My name is written across the front of it in Dominic's steady handwriting. With trembling hands, I tear open the envelope and slip out the card. Only a few words are printed on the thick and smooth stock:

V—

Call me when you get this. I'll be waiting.

—D

I rise from the couch and race back to where I dropped my purse on the floor, fumbling with it until my phone slips out and into my hands. I dial Dominic's number. He picks up on the first ring.

"You got my gift."

"Dominic—what—I—"

He laughs, the sound rich and deep, settling me in spite of myself. "Do you like it?"

"*Half* of it, at least! The other part—"

"I'm assuming you're talking about the plug."

"Yes, the *plug.*" Color surges into my cheeks, even though he can't see me. "That's not the kind of thing I've—I'm not going to—what—"

"Don't fret so much, sweet thing." There's still a layer of laughter under the baritone timbre of his voice. "I gave that to you for an added layer of anticipation, a taste of what's to come—if you decide that you want it."

"Why would I—?" I snap my lips closed, flashing back to the car ride, to the words that tumbled unbidden out of my mouth—*punish me*—and I can feel my entire body blushing at the memory. Oh, God, is *this* what he has in mind?

And why is it making me so wet to imagine it?

"I don't know, Dominic…" But I do know. I *do.*

"You don't have to decide right now." Then his tone shifts gears. "Are you still dressed?"

"Yes, I just got home from the office."

"Let's start with taking off your clothes. Are you ready to follow instructions?"

My shoulders relax. "Yes," I breathe into the phone, finally seeing the game Dominic has set up for us tonight.

"Take them all off, one piece at a time. I'll wait."

CHAPTER EIGHTEEN

Dominic

ER VOICE, EVEN OVER THE PHONE, HAS ME ROCK HARD AND ready.

Anticipation? Yes. A full communication blackout? No. That would have the exact opposite effect of what I'm hoping for.

I can hear fabric dropping to the floor, and then there's a muffled static as Vivienne picks up the phone again.

"Are you naked, sweet thing?"

"I have nothing on."

"Do you have your gifts?"

"No…"

"Get them, and go to your bedroom."

"Okay."

I sense soft footsteps, and then a shifting that tells me she's put the phone between her ear and her shoulder. "I'm going there now."

"How does it feel in your apartment?"

"Empty."

"Temperature-wise."

She laughs a little, low and throaty. "Warm, but not too warm."

"Good."

"I'm in my bedroom."

"Lie down on your bed."

A hushed sound. "I'm lying down."

"Put the plug where you can see it."

"I put it on my bedside table."

"That's perfect."

"Now lay back and close your eyes."

I've locked myself in the penthouse apartment on the twentieth floor of the Wilder Building. I couldn't bear to be on the drive home when she called, because I knew she would call. I *knew* she couldn't stand to wait very long to open the box once she got home. I also know she didn't open it early, because my note would have drawn the truth out of her, driven her to call me even if the workday wasn't over. I know it in my bones without even having to ask her.

"Dominic?"

I've been lost in images of her for too long—the sweet curves of her hips, her soft skin, her full lips on mine—but her voice brings me back. "Are you ready, sweet thing?"

A little laugh. "I don't know what I'm getting ready *for*."

"Pleasure."

She sucks in a little breath. "I thought we were waiting."

"We're waiting for me to make you mine. We don't have to wait for other things." I shift in the leather chair in front of the fireplace, unlit, waiting for the summer to be over, for the bitter winter to come back again. I've taken off my suit jacket and tie, but I wish I could take it all off and stretch out next to Vivienne on her bed. "Are your eyes closed?"

"Yes."

"Touch your collarbone for me. I wish I had my hands on you right now."

She lets out a little sigh. "I wish you did, too."

"Move your hands a little lower. Circle your nipples—use just one finger, sweet thing." Another little breath, a little gasp. "They're hard, aren't they?"

"Oh... yes."

"Sensitive?"

She gulps. "Very."

"Squeeze one of them. Let me hear you feel it." There's a more audible gasp this time. I bet she's soaking wet already, if she wasn't the moment she opened the box and saw what was inside. My cock twitches against the fabric of my pants, but I'm not going to react to it yet. Anticipation.

"I—"

"You don't have to think about it, Vivienne. Just listen to my voice."

This time, her sigh is a satisfied one. This game is one she likes. This game is one *I* like, even if I prefer to play it in-person.

"Slide your hand down your belly."

"How—how far?"

"How far do you think?"

"Should I—?" Her swallow is audible and her voice almost desperate. "Should I touch myself?"

"Should you touch yourself?" I repeat, as if I'm actually considering the words and weighing each one. "Should you slide your hands below your belly button to—oh..." I let my voice trail off.

"What is it?" There's a hint of worry, but her voice is clouded with desire.

"Are you shaved?"

"I—" A nervous giggle. "I got a wax last week."

"Did you leave anything?"

"Just a little...a little landing strip."

"Aha." She's breathing harder now. "Where were we? Should you slip those fingers down over that neat little pussy and find your clit, and circle it with just two fingertips—*exactly* two fingertips, because that's what I'm telling you to do, Vivienne, those are your orders—should you do that? Yes. You should do that."

She exhales, and I know she's been waiting for this.

"It feels good, doesn't it?"

"It feels *so* good."

"Are you wet?"

"*Very* wet."

"If I was with you, I would lick that hot little slit from top to bottom—so slowly—and then I would suck your clit into my mouth and run my tongue over it until you came in my mouth."

The sound she makes next isn't quite a word. It's really more of a moan. We're getting there.

"Take your hand away, Vivienne."

A frustrated growl.

"Are you still touching your hot, wet pussy?"

"No," she groans.

"Pick up the vibrator." A rustle, and then I hear a low hum in the background.

"Oh, Vivienne." I let a hint of disappointment seep into my voice.

"What?" Her tone is anxious, eager.

"I didn't tell you to turn it on."

The humming stops, and Vivienne takes a long moment to speak again. "That was—that was a bad thing to do."

"Yes."

"Will I—will I need to be punished for that?"

She's out on a limb, saying this to me right now, in this moment, when there's no way she can deny it later, there's no way she can say she was so swept up in anything that she just blurted it out without meaning to.

"Oh, yes," I tell her firmly. "Yes, you'll need to be punished." I let that linger, sink in, and hear her breath pick up the pace. "But not right now. Turn on the vibrator."

The hum starts again.

"Slip it down to your pussy, into your folds, and tease yourself with it—lightly, sweet thing, so lightly."

"Oh—"

"Do you want more?"

"*Yes.* Please. I want—I want—"

"Tell me now."

"I want you buried inside me."

"You can't have that right now. But you can put the vibrator in—just a little bit, just how I would tease you with the head of my cock if I was there, make you beg for it." I've waited long enough, and when she gasps again, I unzip my pants. My steel-hard cock springs free, and I take it in my first and begin pumping in a steady rhythm. I can just see her, head thrown back on the pillow, legs spread wide, waiting to fuck herself with the full length of the vibrator.

"Are you listening to me?"

She can barely get the next word out. "Y—yes."

"Thrust it inside, Vivienne. Take all of it in, like you'll take all of me. Do it *hard.*" She gives a little cry, and I know she's done it.

"Are you spread wide for me?"

"As—as wide as I can—I can't go any—"

"Good girl."

She's murmuring my name, and I know she's writhing on her bed, naked and open and exposed, and I tighten my grip on my cock.

"Are you ready to come, sweet thing?"

"Yes. Please, Dominic, *please* say I can come, please—I can't wait much longer, I can't—"

"Wait."

"*Please!*"

Her begging is urgent, sweet, and I'm so close, I'm almost there, I'm right at the edge—

"Come now, Vivienne. *Now.* And let me hear you."

The sound of her moans, the rhythmic rocking of her hips against the bed, pushes me over into abrupt release. At the last moment, I drop the phone on the coffee table and grab a tissue from a discreet dispenser built into its surface, coming in hard waves.

"Now rest," I say, when I'm finally in control of myself again. "Rest, sweet thing."

She murmurs a goodbye, and I hang up.

Not bad for an evening apart.

CHAPTER NINETEEN

Vivienne

DOMINIC MAKES ME WAIT.

It's an exquisite torture, thinking of him, waiting for his text messages to arrive, hoping every moment that I'll step away from my desk and come back to find another one of those white envelopes.

I force myself not to get lost in the fantasies, even though it's an effort that I have to make every hour of every day.

Because I'm here to do a job.

I'm here to do a job that has consequences for the country, as well as for Wilder Enterprises, and even though I'm totally swept up in this man, in waiting for him to make the next move, I can't let myself drown entirely.

Wednesday goes by with no word from him, then Thursday.

After Tuesday's gift, I'm not concerned that he's forgotten me—I'm not worried about that at all. With every moment that goes by, it becomes more and more clear that he's playing this game at a more advanced level than any other man I've known.

I roll my eyes. Not that I've been in relationships like *this* with any other man.

The thought brings me up short as I'm writing up a meeting agenda for Mr. Overhiser.

A relationship?

No.

What am I *thinking*?

I let out a short little laugh, which naturally draws the older man out from his office.

"Vivienne," he says in a jovial tone that somehow manages to seem predatory at the same time. "Care to share?"

"Oh, you know." I give him an indulgent smile. I need him to trust me implicitly, without him getting even the slightest hint that I'm attracted to him in any way. He might be some kind of old lecher outside office hours, but I'm not taking any chances while I work for him. "I was just remembering something funny I saw in a movie last weekend."

"What movie?"

I'm ready with the name of the latest blockbuster hit on the tip of my tongue. Years in the FBI have made this sort of advance preparation habitual, so it's rare that I'm caught off-guard.

By anyone but Dominic.

"That was a good one." He shifts his weight from one foot to another, and I follow up with a close-lipped smile and start to turn my attention back to my computer. "Oh, Vivienne?"

"Yes?" I look up at him with as neutral an expression as possible.

"I'm going to be heading out a few hours early today." A few hours early—it's just past noon. He frowns a little, like he doesn't want to ask me what he's about to ask me. "I'll need you to stay until five."

I wave a hand in the air. "That's no problem. I'm finalizing the meeting agenda for Monday, and then I'll be cross-checking to make sure the schedule is still a green light for the other attendees. Is there anything else you'd like me to take care of before I leave?"

He pretends as if he's just thought of a few more things, but I see right through his act as he reels them off. After the second item on the list, I pull out a notepad and take down careful notes. When he finally stops speaking, I set the notepad down carefully on the desk and glance at my computer screen. "I'll be sure to have that all finished before I leave for the evening."

"Thank you."

"It's absolutely no problem, Mr. Overhiser."

Then he disappears back into his office and I hear him opening various drawers in his desk and file cabinet. Less than a week on the job, and I can already time the swooshes and thuds to the second. This is the sound of Mr. Overhiser leaving for the evening and going God knows where. He has a wife, but from the whispers I overhear around the water cooler, he definitely doesn't spend his evenings with her. One of the other women, Candy, had leaned in close to me on Wednesday afternoon. "I think he's in one of those secret clubs." She'd given me a meaningful look. "You know."

I don't know what kind of secret club she's referring to, but I do know that the city is littered with exclusive clubs for every different taste, and Mr. Overhiser will be going to one that caters to the wealthy.

I wonder if that's where he meets his contact.

Luckily for me, he's presenting me with a prime opportunity on a silver platter.

I hear his voice, speaking low, and know we've reached the end of the "getting ready to leave" performance. He's calling his driver to bring the car around, and then he's striding through the small reception area next to my desk.

"Enjoy your weekend, Vivienne." His eyes linger a little too long on my neckline, which is purposefully high, but his eyes don't stray anywhere else.

I watch him get into the elevator, and then I wait another ten minutes.

I finish the meeting agenda, send an email to all the other chief executive assistants, and then stand up from my desk, bustling around, rearranging papers for the benefit of anyone who might happen to walk by Mr. Overhiser's office.

I step into his main office, put something on the desk, and then step back out again, sitting down at mine for another few minutes. It's a damn elaborate performance, but there's nothing I'm doing that would signal anything out of the ordinary.

When the moment feels right, I slip a flash drive out of my top desk drawer, grab a pile of folders, and head back into his office, sitting down confidently in front of his computer.

I type in his password without hesitating. He only had to enter it in front of me once for me to memorize it. I stick the flash drive into one of the ports, turn my attention to the folder, and wait the fifteen seconds it takes for the drive to work its magic, downloading Overhiser's search history and email logs for the past six months. That should be *more* than enough to determine if there's a connection. It's been three months since this company was flagged by the FBI.

When the download is finished, I take out the flash drive, pile up the folders, and make my way back to my desk, sitting down just in time for the desk phone to ring.

My heart is only beating slightly harder.

"Mr. Overhiser's office." My voice is smooth, betraying absolutely nothing.

"Vivienne."

One word and my entire body is alight with desire. "Mr. Wilder." I have to be careful in my response, because the door is open to the rest of the offices and half the executive assistants are as gossip-obsessed as Marie. "What can I do for you?"

"Are you hungry?"

I'd been expecting a thousand other responses, most having to do with the sensual and sexy things he'd like to do with me—and *to* me—but this one throws me for a loop.

"Am I—um, I haven't eaten yet."

"Are your responsibilities taken care of for the lunch hour?"

"Of course." I inject a little insult into my tone. "I'm ahead of schedule, in fact." *More than you know...*

"Come have lunch with me."

"In your office?"

"In my penthouse. The elevator will ask you for a code. It's 1123."

It's been three days since I've spoken to him. There's no decision to be made.

"I'm on my way."

CHAPTER TWENTY

Dominic

VIVIENNE STEPS OFF THE ELEVATOR WITH FLUSHED CHEEKS and a sway in her hips, her green eyes determined. Still, she's smiling all the same, a private smile that makes me wish I could read her thoughts, just this moment.

"You kept me waiting." Her voice falls gently in the quiet space, here on top of the building, where the only sound to keep us company is the hum of the air conditioning unit and the wind swirling around the building. We're a week into July and the city is sultry and hot, but up here, it's cool and dark.

"You enjoyed yourself." I don't pose it as a question because it's obvious from the look on her face that she *has* been enjoying herself.

"Well," she says, crossing the room and coming to stand in

front of me. I've taken a position in the center, near a small dining table set for two with a white linen tablecloth, one edge neatly pressed against the window glass so we can look out over the view while we eat. "You *did* give me a gift that made it easy to...find enjoyable pockets of time."

Not that I intend to spend much time looking at the view when Vivienne is seated right across from me.

I lean down to speak directly into her ear, even though there's nobody else to hear us, and I've made sure we won't be interrupted. "Doesn't the anticipation taste wonderful?"

"No," she says, and then her hands are on the sides of my face, pulling me in for a kiss that starts out hard and hot and builds in passion until she breaks away abruptly. "But you—*you* taste like heaven."

I could have said the same thing to her, but I don't say anything. I reach out and trace the line of her jaw with a fingertip, and she leans her head into my hand, her eyes locked on mine. "It's hard to wait, Dominic." Her voice is a husky whisper, and when I speak, mine is, too.

"You only have to wait a little longer."

A flash of frustration crosses her face, a flash of need. "How much longer?"

That's my cue. I wrap my hands around her jaw and pull her face into mine, kissing her in a way that demands submission, that demands that she open for me, and she does. I back her up against a partial wall behind the table, pressing her spine against the smooth surface, and when she reaches for me, I catch both of her wrists in one hand, pinning them above her head. Her nipples are pebbled even through the fabric of her bra and her dress, and with the other hand, I toy with one, then the other, drawing out a gasp from her that turns into a little moan.

I press the length of my body against hers, and her hips rise away from the wall to meet me, my hard length pressing into the front of her smooth belly.

"I'll decide when you've waited long enough," I growl into her ear, and every breath she takes is a testament to how turned on she is. "Or do you want to push me? Do you want to keep asking until you've crossed the line, until I'm forced to punish you?"

Her head is tipped back against the wall, her elegant neck exposed to me, but at my words, her eyes fly open and something wicked bolts through them. Her lips part. "How long, Dominic?" Each word is a separate island falling from her mouth. "How long do I have to wait?"

I steel my face, drowning in the intensity of her eyes, and her eyebrows raise a fraction of an inch. She wants this. She wants it badly, but now that the moment is here—now that she sees the future in my face—nervousness has to be cascading through her veins.

I give a short nod, then draw her hands down in front of her. "You've made your choice, Vivienne. Come this way."

I don't give her much of a choice, leading her by the wrists away from the table and into the private office, where the gleaming mahogany desk awaits. I stop her right in front of it.

"Bend over."

She bites her lip, cutting her eyes sideways at me. I look back at her, unwavering. This is part of the pleasure of punishment, as she's about to learn. She opens her mouth, then closes it again.

"Not fast enough," I say tersely. "That will only add to your punishment. Bend. Over."

She moves to the desk, but it's still not quick enough, so I put a hand on her shoulders and press. Vivienne gasps as the pressure forces her to bend.

"Hands on the desk. Head down—closer. There. Arch your back." I run my hands down her back, adjusting her position. "Your legs should be spread." She moves them apart a few inches. "Wider." I bend to growl into her ear. "This is punishment, Vivienne, and you'll be exposed to me whether you like it or not."

"Yes—yes, Dominic."

My cock gets harder at her attempt.

"'Yes, sir.'"

"Yes, sir."

I press my hand harder into the small of her back. "Hold this position."

She's trembling under my hands, but her voice is clear. "Yes, sir."

I flip the skirt of her dress upward, folding it toward her hips, displaying her black lace panties to me. Then I draw the palm of my hand across the luscious curves of her ass.

"Ten strokes, with my open hand," I say, as if I'm commenting on the weather. "Five for insisting on asking the question after I told you to stop, and five more for resisting your punishment."

She opens her mouth as if she's going to argue, but thinks better of it. Her hands go tight on the edge of the desk, her knuckles white, but her ass lifts another inch into the air. I have to force myself not to dip my fingers into her folds right now, but from the scent of her, she's already wet.

I hook my fingers into the waistband of her panties and pull them down. She gasps as the air curls its tendrils between her legs, and the sound makes my cock twitch in my pants. But I'm not going to indulge it yet. No—that's not the lesson here.

I take my place beside her, one hand on the small of her back, and rub my other hand over her ass one more time. "Count."

Then, without another moment of hesitation, I whip my hand back and bring it down hard on one of her cheeks. The sound of my hand connecting with her creamy flesh, turning it pink, makes me want to come right now.

Vivienne yelps, but then she remembers the rules, and *damn,* does she want to play the game. "One."

I bring my hand down again, another crack. "Two..." she whimpers.

I don't think she's ever been spanked before—not like this—but her whole body is tensed with the effort of staying still.

"Good girl."

I bring my hand down a third time, and watch a droplet of her juices trickle down her inner thigh.

CHAPTER TWENTY-ONE

Vivienne

Dominic Wilder is spanking me, bringing his hand down in even strokes across my ass, and my heart is thundering in my chest. The air in the room has thinned, somehow, and I can hardly get a breath, but somehow I manage to suck one in just in time to count the next stroke.

I can't believe how turned on I am.

I can't *believe* how dirty this is, how filthy, how much I like it. I can't believe that I didn't turn around and run the moment I let that fantasy slip out of my mouth to him, and I can't believe I didn't laugh it off earlier when he let me know I was goading him into punishment.

And when he says "*Good girl...*"

I hold tightly to the desk like it's a lifeboat, counting. Five, six, seven, and my mind roils with the stinging pain, the thought of my own ass turning red under the force of his hand, the way he must look standing next to me, so tall, so powerful, and here I am, legs spread wide, bent over a desk, ass in the air, *submitting* to a man I can't get out of my head.

My thoughts are crystallized with each stroke, and then they fly apart in the interval. Heat pulses in my cheeks. I'm mortified, but I don't know if I'm embarrassed because I wanted this, or because I'm enjoying it right now, or both.

How could I be enjoying this? I'm an independent woman. I've worked hard for everything I have. I've challenged men in my job and I'm making a name for myself with or without them. And here I am—here I am—bent over Dominic Wilder's desk having practically begged him to punish me.

And it feels—

It hurts, but the ache zings up and down my spine, turning into a need so intense it's all I can do not to buck my hips, not to beg him to touch me, to please, *please,* let me come. I can feel my wetness dripping down the insides of my thighs, and it's a dead giveaway—there's no way he hasn't noticed.

Eight, nine, ten.

There's a ringing silence when he's done spanking me, and my entire body trembles, hands still gripping the edge of the desk. I hold my breath. I don't want to move, don't want the moment to shatter. If I have to sit down across from him and eat lunch right now, I think I'll die.

Then Dominic is touching me again, his smooth palm rubbing over the hot skin on my bottom, gentle, firm, and I can't stop the moan that escapes me.

"Oh—"

"You've been a *very* good girl," he says, his voice low and measured and soft. "You took your punishment well. And I see—" Finally— *finally*—his hand is sliding backward, and I press my ass out toward him, spreading my legs apart another inch, a wordless cry that I need him, I *need* him. "I see you've enjoyed it."

"Yes—" The word is a hiss that's drawn out by the fact that he's stroking my wet, swollen slit, his fingers dancing over my folds. "*Please*—"

"What do you want from me, sweet thing?"

"I—" I want him to fuck me, but I know the game we're playing, and I don't think all the begging in the world will convince him to take me right now. In fact, begging might have the opposite effect. I can't get my thoughts in order to figure out what to say. I can't— "I want you to fuck me," I blurt out. "I want you to, please, God, I want you to, but I know—"

"You know I'm not going to give in, don't you?"

"I know—" Now my hips are bucking against his hand. I can't control them, can't do anything but hold on tight to the desk, stay bent over, pray that he'll touch me, give me some release. If he's not going to, I might have to quit the game, because my core is throbbing with need, aching. "I need to come. Dominic, *please*, you're torturing me."

"Sweet thing, I would never do that." The instant the words are out of his mouth, his hands increase in pressure, two fingers slipping into my wet channel. My pussy clenches hard around them, and I gasp at how good it feels to be reacting to his touch, how good it feels to have something inside of me, even if he won't fuck me yet, damn him, *damn* him.

He comes to stand behind me, the other hand sliding around the front of my hips and pulling me back a few inches, making space. His fingers find my clit, and the moment they do, my head falls back and I cry out. "Oh, *fuck—*"

"Do what you need to do, sweet thing."

As soon as I have his permission, I give myself over. I give myself over to the fact that he's fucking me with his fingers, sliding another one in, twisting them and hooking them to find parts of me that send searing jolts of pleasure so powerful through every nerve ending that the desk is all I have grounding me to the world. I'm pulsing around those fingers, as he circles my clit with his fingertips in a relentless rhythm, my hips jerking forward to those fingers and then back onto the others, and all of it is slick and hot and I've never been to such dizzying heights of pleasure in all my life. The orgasm that hits me in the next moment is so powerful that I scream, realizing too late that someone could hear, but I can't stop, I can't stop the heat pouring over me, burning me, making me new.

When it's over, Dominic is there, whispering sweet nothings until I catch my breath.

But I'm not done yet.

I straighten up, leaving my black panties around my ankles, and turn to face him. A twitch in one of the muscles near his mouth gives him away, the look in his eyes, a barely controlled burning—

I move before he can stop me, before he can say no.

I drop to my knees, reaching for his belt buckle, undoing the clasp in an instant, and pull his zipper down. His cock springs free as soon as the zipper stops containing it, and I can't help but gasp again. It's thick and perfect and ramrod straight.

"Vivienne—"

"It's your turn." I inject every ounce of firmness into my voice, and then I take him in both my hands and lean forward, sucking the head in first, softly, delicately, and then swirling my tongue around his shaft, taking him in inch by inch until he's pressed up against my throat, the sensation slightly alarming and unbelievably hot. I suck and swirl, his hands coming down heavily on my shoulders, until he explodes into my mouth, hips jerking, teeth gritted, his own low guttural moan reverberating in the confines of the room.

My entire body is warm and loose as I stand up, tugging my panties back in place, rising up on tiptoes to kiss his jawline, watch him try to catch his breath.

"Okay," I say, and his eyebrows raise in a question. "*Now* I'm ready for lunch."

CHAPTER TWENTY-TWO

Dominic

THE CALL FROM CHRIS O'CONNOR COMES ONLY MOMENTS after Vivienne steps into the elevator, and for a split second, I think it's her, calling to murmur something dirty into my ear before she goes back to Overhiser's office for the rest of the day. My heart sinks when I see the number on the caller ID.

"What happened?"

Chris wouldn't be calling me direct for nothing.

"Hey, Dominic."

"Just start talking, Chris." I'd forgotten about the FBI business during that lunch break, and I'd been planning to sit in front of the fireplace for a good fifteen minutes with a glass of something dark and alcoholic and lose myself in the memory of Vivienne's lips wrapped around my cock, her hot wet mouth working me until I came…and more than that, the fiery determination in her eyes that we be on the same level, that I get at least what I gave…pleasure.

It makes my heart ache.

She was practically glowing at lunch, beaming, and I felt the same way, like I'd finally found someone who's an equal despite our vastly different job titles and net worth, someone who's concerned about *fairness,* of all things, and isn't just here to leech off of me.

Or, maybe I'm being a fool and she is someone I can't see through. Maybe she *is* playing some kind of game to get rich from dating a billionaire, but I don't think so. She might have other secrets that can only be revealed with time, but Vivienne Davis isn't a gold digger.

So it's not Chris O'Connor I want to be talking to right now.

"Testy, testy," he says, sounding a little hurt.

"I've got a busy schedule. Do you have news for me?" He *could* be calling to tell me the investigation is off, in which case I've been a total asshole to him for nothing. The beat's worth of silence tells me everything I need to know. "Where do you want to meet?"

"Same bar as last time?"

No. Too risky. I don't want this to become a habit—for Chris's sake and mine.

"Where are you?"

"A block away from HQ." He names a street and cross street.

"One of my drivers will pick you up in five minutes. I know where we can go."

* * *

Twenty minutes later, we're seated in a private room of a club with such a high membership price tag that most of New York—even its elite—doesn't know about it. I rarely put it to use—I've spent most of the last few years in my office, so there's been no need for confidential meetings in a place like this—but in a pinch, it's nice to have a secure location that isn't a dive bar.

Chris shifts in his seat. The room we're in features a picture window that doesn't offer much of a view, but at least it lets in streams of daylight. A waitress in a form-fitting uniform has swept in with a tray, setting out various appetizers—delicately crafted sushi rolls and other small bites that I want despite just having finished lunch—and backs out again without a word once she's set two tumblers of whiskey in front of us.

He takes a deep breath, then picks up the glass and sips at it. "I thought you meant another bar."

"Are you going to complain, old friend?"

One corner of his mouth rises into a smile. "No, but this kind of place—"

"Is the kind of place you should get to know, if you're going to keep giving me confidential information I shouldn't have."

"Fair point." He draws one of the appetizer plates toward him and chooses from the serving plates in the center of the table. "I wanted to stay in contact."

I pick up a slim section of sushi and pop it into my mouth. The flavor explodes onto my tongue, the fish so fresh it was probably swimming around moments ago. "Do you *not* have any new developments?"

He flicks his eyes upward, then back down at the food. "The department isn't very interested in you anymore."

"Good. I'm not selling tech secrets to the Chinese government, so that makes a great deal of sense."

"Unfortunately, our undercover agent isn't making much headway. It might—it might take a little longer than I thought, and I wanted to keep you in the loop. Even though I shouldn't." He gives me a pointed look, like he needs to remind me that he's doing me a favor.

"And, what, you missed our little chats from college days?" This is all information he could have given me over the phone—not nearly the caliber of what he told me in a damn bar not too long ago. "Jesus, Chris. I thought this was a real update."

"It *is,* in that we're moving on from you as a prime suspect. You should be relieved. Selling information like this when you have government contracts is a huge fucking deal."

I sigh. "I know. I'm sorry. I've just—I've had some different things on my mind lately."

Chris's eyes light up. "Damn it, Wilder, did you meet a woman and not tell me?"

I narrow my eyes, appraising him from across the table. I shouldn't be telling anyone about Vivienne, but how far could it possibly go? It's Chris, for God's sake, and we're within the walls of one of the safest rooms in the city. "You could say that."

"Is that why you're suddenly *irritated* to find out more information about the FBI investigation that's happening right under your nose?"

"Hell yes," I tell him with a stupid grin. "I was thinking about her when you called. You interrupted me."

"She must be pretty special if she can take your mind off an FBI investigation. You were pissed as hell when I first told you."

"She is. She—" I can't find words that do Vivienne justice. "I only met her a few weeks ago, but man—"

"Who is this woman?"

I raise a finger into the air, chastising him. "No details."

He scoffs. "Oh, come on. Like I'm going to know her."

For an instant, I debate telling him Vivienne's name, that she started at my company a few weeks ago, that I want her badly, that right now the only place I want to be is in her arms.

I shake my head. "Not until we've...figured things out."

"Oh, it's like *that*?" Understanding settles over Chris's face.

"It's like that."

I take another bite of sushi. My heart is warm at the thought of Vivienne, but I'm not filled with rage. I'm not anxious to get back to the Wilder Building and stalk the halls until I find whoever it is that's stealing from me. Instead, I feel...calm. I feel willing to let the FBI do its job, to let my friend on the inside keep me updated.

The realization is like a shock of cold water. For the first time in years, there's something more important to me than Wilder Enterprises.

And it's Vivienne Davis.

"So—is that all the news?" I'm ravenous again, suddenly, wholly, and I lean forward and start loading an appetizer plate with some of everything.

"Yeah…" Chris looks at me with wide eyes. "You okay, man?"

"More than okay. Let's drink."

CHAPTER TWENTY-THREE

Vivienne

THE LUNCH DATE WITH DOMINIC UNLEASHES A TORRENT OF text messages that last all weekend—the kind of questions I would have asked a high school boyfriend, my heart beating fast awaiting every answer. We trade them in rapid-fire bursts, though he doesn't suggest another date—not yet. I get the impression we're sandwiched between playing the anticipation game and getting serious, and I can't get enough of it.

But I have to cut myself off at intervals during the day, because the weekend is my best shot at finding out what Mr. Overhiser is *really* up to.

I send some of the data to the team at FBI headquarters, but I sift through the rest myself. Someone else might not understand everything that's being discussed in these messages, and I want to nail this. I scour hundreds of emails and flip through log after log of websites pulled from his browser—even those he deleted—looking for any connection to someone outside the company, any information being exchanged with a person who shouldn't have access.

It's a little like being in the Executive Support Department again, only I'm doing it in sweatpants and running clothes, allowing myself breaks only to eat and run through Central Park when I'm feeling at the end of my rope.

What's your favorite color?

The message from Dominic comes in while I'm eating a bowl of Lucky Charms over the sink. I crave them when I'm in the middle of time-intensive projects, and this one definitely qualifies.

I don't want to say...

I'm not really embarrassed about it, but when I'm not up to my eyeballs in an old man's emails, I'm letting myself get swept along by the open, flirty tone of the texts. I'm bathing in it, basking in it. The only thing that could be better would be to whisper these questions directly into Dominic's ear.

Are you...are you serious?

There's something about his personality via text that makes me *like* him. I was attracted to him the moment I saw him, even though I knew it was a mistake, and the way I feel when the sensation of his hands on my body comes to mind. Through the phone, I'm seeing his playful side, and I really, *really* like it. I like *him*.

I'm serious.

My playful side can't be contained with an iPhone in my hands, either.

Is it something disgusting? Like the color of rotten eggs?

Aren't rotten eggs just yellow?

Green, too, probably. Not that I've ever seen any.

It's pink.

There's a long pause, so long it has to be purposeful.

Pink.

Yes.

Your favorite color is pink?

Sue me. No, don't...I can't afford a good lawyer!

Mine is purple.

I pause for exactly as long as it takes to send back five emojis that look like they're laughing hysterically. He doesn't answer.

You're serious?? Dominic Wilder's favorite color is purple?

I'll buy you a thousand purple dresses to prove it.

That doesn't prove anything...but I'll take the dresses.

Is your closet big enough?

Could you send a closet along with them?

Your wish is my command, sweet thing.

Heat comes to my cheeks at the phrase, and I put the phone down, finishing the last of the cereal in my bowl. Lucky Charms are so damn good. I don't know why I deny myself this small pleasure except during times of stress. Maybe I should stop. Denying myself pleasure, even when it's risky as hell, has not been my number one priority lately.

I rinse the bowl in the sink, looking over at the phone every few moments to see if Dominic has anything else to say, but it looks like we're entering a lull.

Which is convenient because I need a shower.

I ran a hard six miles in Central Park before I ate the cereal, and my clothes are clinging to my skin. I strip them off and toss them into the laundry hamper in the bathroom, jump into the shower, and try to push Dominic out of my mind.

What am I missing when it comes to Overhiser?

After the shower, I spend another two hours in front of my computer, coming up empty-handed.

I pop up a bowl of popcorn, grab a bottle of wine and a glass, and then stew on my couch for the rest of the evening, until, at last, just as I'm falling asleep, I come up with another plan.

＊ ＊ ＊

I get to the office early on Monday morning, careful to arrange my face into a bit of a grimace, and hustle to my desk. The computer starts up with a hum, and as soon as I've signed in, I put a flash drive into one of the ports. It's a different flash drive than I used on Overhiser's machine—this one carefully marked with a red star on the side—and it breaks my computer, just a little.

I let out a heavy sigh, dropping the flash drive back in my purse and putting the purse in my bottom drawer, which I lock before stalking back down the hall to the elevator.

Tech Support is housed in the basement, which is no surprise.

It's the easiest space to control the temperature, and Wilder Enterprises, of course, has more than a few internal servers to power the company. Not that I'm an expert. I know just enough to be dangerous, and hopefully bail myself out of what's quickly coming to seem like a dead end.

At first, when I step off the elevator at Basement Level 1, I think it's empty. The silence is heavy, broken only by the whir of the stacks of servers positioned against one wall. There isn't a single light turned on in any of the offices along the other wall, and I let out a little sigh, ready to turn around and head back up to my floor.

Just as I'm about to turn for the elevator, there's movement at one of the doors. A figure appears out of the dark, and I have to stifle a gasp.

"Oh, my God," the man says, a shadow falling over his face. "I'm—I'm sorry. Can I help you?"

My heart is pounding in my chest. Why the hell is he down here with no lights on? His hands are full of the kinds of blue folders we use up on the executive level.

"I'm Vivienne Davis," I say, trying to steady myself on the sound of my own voice. "My—my computer is having some kind of problem, and I was wondering if you could check it out from here..."

I want to look over his shoulder while he signs in, but this guy is going to be a miss—I can already tell. He shifts the folders in his hands. "I can come up in a few minutes and look. That's—that's usually the first step," he says. I can't quite see his eyes, and it's unsettling as hell to me.

"Okay. Thanks. I'm working for Mr. Overhiser." I finish it off with a little laugh, like this whole thing is a little absurd, but the sound just falls into more silence.

"I'll be there."

I turn on my heel and go.

CHAPTER TWENTY-FOUR

Dominic

MY OWN GAME IS WORKING AGAINST ME, BECAUSE BY Monday morning, I'm bursting out of my skin. The only thing that managed to slake my thirst for her was the fact that we texted each other constantly all weekend.

Everything grates on my nerves all day. Every meeting drags on into eternity. Every point that my executives pause to discuss makes me want to pound my fist on the table and tell them to stop wasting my time.

By four, I'm done.

Something has to give, and I sink into the chair behind my desk and rub at my temples. Something has to give, because I can't maintain this level of obsession with both Wilder Enterprises *and* Vivienne.

But there's a fine line to walk. I can't let my attention waver. That's what my father did, and that's what got him a dead wife and ruined his reputation in New York City and, for all I know, the rest of the world. I *don't* want that.

I also don't want to lose my tenuous grasp on Vivienne.

Maybe it's not so tenuous, though. Maybe what we have is the first real thing I've had in my life in years.

I want to see her. I want to be with her, and I don't want to play any more games. I've stretched the tension to a breaking point, and my nerves are beginning to fray. The text messages aren't enough. They're just not enough. I need to *be* with her, somewhere private, somewhere alone.

My penthouse seems like the perfect place. The *only* place I can realistically think of going without fueling up my private jet, which just strikes me as a hassle, one on top of another.

"Emily!" I stand up from behind my desk at the exact moment she appears in the doorway. "I'm done for the day."

Her eyes widen, but only for a split second. "I'll cancel the last meeting of the day."

"Move it to Wednesday."

"Wednesday?"

It's like she wants to confirm that I don't actually mean *Tuesday*. It wasn't that long ago when I planned an extensive vacation and cancelled it three days in. She's probably wondering if I'm going off the rails right now instead, if she should have tried to gently insist that I stay away for at least a week. But Emily would never do that.

"Wednesday. And push everything else for tomorrow to later in the week."

She gives a little nod and turns away, the sound of fingers tapping her keyboard floating through the door a moment later.

There's not much to bring with me—I don't have an overcoat in the middle of the summer—so it's a matter of taking my phone out of my pocket, texting my driver, and walking out.

In the elevator I send another message, this one to Vivienne.

You can tell me if your boss is gone for the day.

It's just flirty enough to disguise the fact that I'm over this day, I'm over Wilder Enterprises, I'm over everything but her. Her reply comes in a few moments later, before I've reached the lobby.

How'd you know? :)

That old bastard thinks I don't know that he never stays past four unless I've called a meeting. Come meet me.

I don't know. He did ask me to stay until five.

He asked you to stay until five so you could cover his ass if I called the office.

Really??

That last one makes me laugh.

Come meet me. One block down, in front of the coffee shop with the stupid logo.

You mean...the one with the hot pink mug?

That's the one.

Her next message is a thumbs-up emoji.

I slide into the back seat of the Town Car, which seems to have been ready and waiting for me already—there's not a hint of the sticky July heat in the interior. I tell Craig, the driver, where to go, and he pulls out into traffic without making his usual small talk. The look on my face must be enough to tell him that I'm not in the mood for conversation.

Ten minutes later, Vivienne pulls open the back door to the Town Car, her light, flowery scent wafting in on the breeze, and slides in next to me. She pulls the door closed behind her, gives a little nod to the driver, and slips her hand into mine.

"I missed you over the weekend."

I give her a grin. "How could you have missed me? We were on the phone the entire time." It's a damn coy thing to say, and it reminds me of being in college, of the endless flirtation that would go on with some women before they'd go to bed with you, how the cute quickly became cloying. With Vivienne, I don't think it ever will.

"We were." She looks me in the eyes, and then decides something based on what she sees there. It only takes her a moment to scoot closer and lay her head on my shoulder. "Purple?" Her voice is soft, and I can't see her face, but I hear the smile in her voice.

I squeeze her shoulders, then slide my arm down around her waist. "I'm done waiting," I murmur into her hair. "I'm done playing games."

She tenses under my arm, then relaxes again. "Thank *God.* Even that vibrator hasn't been able to keep up with me the last few days."

I close my eyes and breathe her in, relishing the thought of her spread open and teasing herself, face pink with exertion and desire, almost hearing the little sounds she'd have been making while she got herself off over and over again.

Next to me, she sucks in a little breath. "Dominic, you have to wait a little longer." Her hand brushes over the bulge in my pants, and I cover my mouth with my hand, then lower my fingers to her lips.

"Not much longer."

"No?"

"Absolutely not." I shift in the seat, trying to get comfortable, and resign myself to the fact that I'm not *going* to be comfortable, not until Vivienne is riding my cock into a powerful orgasm. "But I do have to ask you a question."

She pulls back a little, frowning at me, her green eyes going a little darker. "What is it?"

I lean in close. "It's a very serious question, and I'm going to need you to think carefully before you answer."

She blinks a couple of times, her breath speeding up. She reaches for my hand again and holds it tightly. "Dominic," she says, her tone urgent. "What is it?"

I look her straight in the eye, keeping my face collected and serious. "Will you go home with me?"

Her mouth drops open, and then she laughs out loud. "You're terrible."

"You love it."

"Maybe I do." Then she leans in close, until her lips are brushing my earlobe—a page right out of my own playbook—and drops her voice so that I'm the only one who hears her next words. "But I'm only going home with you if you promise to fuck me. Today. Not tomorrow, not another day, but *today*. I need it, Dominic. I need *you*."

I take her face in my hands and pull her in close. Before I cover her mouth with mine, I give her the answer she wants. "Yes. It's time. I swear."

CHAPTER TWENTY-FIVE

Vivienne

I CAN'T KEEP MY HANDS OR MY MOUTH AWAY FROM DOMINIC FOR the rest of the ride to wherever it is we're going, which turns out to be an understated building on the Upper East Side. By the time the Town Car pulls up to the curb, my entire body is like one raw nerve, and we've long since stopped saying anything to one another. He gently lifts me upright from where I've been leaning against the door, his powerful torso covering mine, and reaches to help me straighten the skirt of the gray shift dress I wore to the office today before exiting the vehicle.

The driver comes around to open the door and helps me step out, and when I've gotten my footing on the curb, I can tell he's trying not to smile. I give him a big grin. "*Thank* you..."

"Craig." He sticks out his hand, and I shake it firmly.

"I'm Vivienne."

He winks at me. "I know."

Then Dominic's hand is on the small of my back, steering me through the thick summer heat toward the lobby of his building.

Unlike Wilder Enterprises, there's nothing ostentatious about the lobby, nothing to hint that a member of the country's richest social class resides here. Dominic steps forward, leading me past a bank of two elevators and around the corner to a third, this one with a keypad next to the call button. He punches in a code, then turns to look down into my eyes, his gaze smoldering. My breath hitches.

"Even the elevator takes too long today."

"I know exactly what you mean." I intertwine my fingers with his and hold on tight, wanting to pull him down for another kiss but knowing that if I do, we might never make it up to his apartment. "You have a *lot* of private elevators."

"Just two." He shakes his head, then nods another time, remembering. "No. Three."

"What more could a girl ask for?"

His eyes dance with his smile. "I'd say a lot more than elevators. Why don't I show you?"

"Oh, *please* do." Every word out of his mouth is so charged that even when we're talking about building transportation technology, I get wet. *Wetter*, if I'm being honest about it, because my panties are already soaked from the ride here.

The doors glide open as the elevator arrives, and we both step in, Dominic jamming his finger on the button for the penthouse.

"Wow," I say, squeezing his hand. "The penthouse!"

He says nothing, but as the doors glide closed, he wraps his hands around my waist and presses me up against the wall of the elevator, the surface cold through my dress, and I shiver with pleasure as he bends his head down to kiss my collarbone. His hands work at the buttons at the front of my dress, deftly undoing one, two, three buttons, and then he's yanking down the dress and my bra, exposing one breast, then the other, to the cool air as the elevator rises.

I press the palms of my hands back against the wall of the elevator, and his mouth makes contact with my nipples, already hard and straining for him, a heated, swirling pleasure that's arcing down my spine as he swirls his tongue over one pebbled nub, the pad of his thumb circling the other.

"Do you like that?" he says softly, and something about the question strikes me as so vulnerable, so open, that my heart bursts into a thousand pieces. The sheer need sweeping through my veins repairs itself in an instant.

"*Yes.* Please—" I raise one hand and curl my fingers through his thick, dark hair, putting the slightest amount of pressure there so that he doesn't lift his head, doesn't leave me.

My nipples are on fire from his attention, and he's working his way back up my neck when the doors of the elevator open directly into his apartment.

I hardly see any of it—the expensive furniture in the sunken living room, a kitchen gleaming with top-of-the-line appliances that look like they've never been used—because the moment we're inside, Dominic gets to work.

"Hands over your head, sweet thing." I raise my arms without a moment of hesitation. He slips my dress up over my head. My bra is barely hanging on as it is, and he finishes removing it and drops it to the floor next to my dress.

Then Dominic kneels on the carpet in front of me, running his hands over the thin silk fabric of my panties. He pulls my hips toward his face, breathes in my scent, and hooks his fingers in the waistband, slowly drawing them down to my knees, and then my ankles.

I step out of those, too.

From his position on the floor, Dominic looks up into my eyes, his own filled with lustful need and power and something else, something stronger. "You're gorgeous." His voice emerges as a raw whisper.

"So are you."

I can't help but touch his upturned face, running my fingers through his hair, and he leans forward and presses his lips against my landing strip. The slightest touch sets me ablaze, and I throw my head back, sucking in a breath.

"Spread for me, sweet thing." I move my legs apart, and he draws two fingers down my slit. "You're so ready for me."

"*Yes.*" The word comes out as a moan, a plea.

He puts his fingers in his mouth and sucks. "Mmm. I have to have more of that. Hold on…"

I brace myself on his shoulders, and the next instant his mouth is on me, licking, delving into my folds, sucking at my clit, lapping up all of the juices that have collected. His hands are firm on my hips, holding me in place, and oh, God—oh *God*—it's a good thing, because my knees go weak from the pleasure consuming me, from his tongue diving in deep, from his fingers sliding in and out of my slick channel, fucking me while he swirls his tongue over my clit and draws it into his mouth, creating a suction that makes my legs quiver.

He's relentless, *relentless*, and I can't stop myself, I can't control the way the air brushes teasingly against my nipples, the way his fingers fill me and tease me and torment me as he draws them slowly in and out, and I come hard into his mouth, my feet barely keeping contact with the floor.

When I open my eyes, Dominic is standing, stripping off his jacket, his shirt, his tie, wiping his mouth with his sleeve, looking at me with a passionate fire glowing in his eyes, and I can hardly get a breath because this is *just* getting started. And I want more of him, want to run my fingers down his washboard abs that I'm finally getting to see, want him to claim me, want to finally be *his*.

CHAPTER TWENTY-SIX

Dominic

VIVIENNE IS PURE SWEETNESS, AND I COULD WORSHIP HER naked body and its pure womanly curves standing in my foyer for the rest of my life, if I didn't desperately need to fuck her right now. Her face is pink with the afterglow of her first orgasm of the afternoon, and her nipples stand out dark and desperate, and I reach out to cup her breasts in the palms of my hands. She lets her head tilt back, breathing hard and fast. Her whole body is trembling, and I kiss her once on the lips, her softness giving way to me, and then I scoop her up in my arms.

It's not far to the master suite, and when I get there, I lay her gently on the bed. She curls her arms up above her head, arching back, and when she speaks her voice is low, saturated with need.

"Please, Dominic. I need—"

"I need to fuck you." There is no more time for playing games. There is no more time for anticipation, for waiting, for drawing this out, delicious as it's been. We're there. We're at the moment when anticipation turns into pure agony, and I'm going to take it in my hands and turn it into sheer pleasure. I undo my belt, unzip my pants, and strip all the rest of my clothes off, then climb onto the bed and position my body over Vivienne.

"Spread wide for me." She emits a little hitched breath, but she obeys, even though I think we both know this isn't a *game* anymore, this isn't a little interlude in my office, this is *real.* I have the sense that she wants to lose herself in me, just as much as I want to lose myself in her, and I'm willing to take control only as far as she needs me to in this moment.

She's already so wet, and a new gush of her sweet juices glides over my fingers when I stroke her folds, hooking my fingers to the front, playing her like a violin. Vivienne lets out a low groan, her hips bucking up from the bedspread, and she reaches for me, her hands framing both sides of my face, drawing me down for a kiss.

She crushes her lips against mine, her tongue thrusting into my mouth, and that's when I *know.*

I love Vivienne Davis.

I *love* her.

She wants that balance. She wants me to be who I am—powerful and in control and willing to take over when she wants to let go for a while. But she's also damn powerful in her own right. She's not afraid to take what she wants, and what she wants right now is me. Vivienne is wet for me, soaking for me, and the desperate searching of her tongue is all I need to leave every last moment of waiting behind.

I break the kiss, pulling back, and slide my arms underneath her, flipping her onto her hands and knees with a quick movement. She braces herself, automatically raising her ass into the air, lowering her head to the pillow, and I spread her creamy thighs with my hands and blow onto her folds, eliciting a low hiss.

"*Yes,* yes, yes. *Please,* Dominic, *please...*"

Her begging is the prettiest sound I've ever heard. I line up my thickness with her slit, put my hands on her hips, and pull her backward until the head of my cock is right up against her slick opening. She wriggles in my hands, trying to force herself backward onto me, but I hold her in place.

"You're mine, Vivienne Davis. *Mine.*"

"I'm yours," she gasps, and as her fingers clutch at the bedspread, I slam my full length inside of her.

She lets out a little scream that's all pleasure, and it mixes with the low sound I hear coming from my chest. Vivienne is tight, her muscles pulsing around my cock as I pound inside her again and again. It's like she was made for me. I tunnel as deep as I can go, bottoming out, and her hips are like a jackhammer, jerking with every thrust.

"I—" Vivienne gasps, unable to get the words out, and I plunge in as deep as I can go and then hold still. Instinctively, she lowers her breasts another inch toward the bed. She's trembling so hard under my hands, my cock buried inside of her, that I can't believe she's staying in this position. "I—"

"You don't need my permission to come, sweet thing. Come on my cock, baby. *Come.*"

She explodes around me, crying out again and again, and the force of her muscles pulsating around me pushes me over the edge. I come hard inside her, impaling her fully on my cock, as the aftershocks rock through her body, again and again.

We stay frozen for a moment, and then she curls to the side, pulling me down with her. Her flushed face is the picture of blissful satisfaction, and my heart breaks. I run a hand through her hair, never wanting to look away from her eyes ever again. I lean down closer to her, and I say it, I say it out loud, even though there are a million reasons not to. "I love you, Vivienne Davis."

Her gasp this time is sheer delight, and she wraps one hand around the back of my head and pulls me down, kissing me with a tenderness I don't think I've come up against in years, if ever. "I love *you*, Dominic. It's—" She shakes her head.

"It's risky," I murmur. "There are a thousand reasons not to be together. But I love you. And that's the only reason I need. It's the only thing I need to know."

She's silent for a moment, and then she lets her eyes travel down the length of my body. "You're *kidding.*" Her voice is still low and soft, but her eyes are dancing and glittering.

"That's how much I want you." My cock is already standing at attention again, just from breathing in her intoxicating scent, just from stroking my fingers down over the curves of her breasts.

And Vivienne, with a grin that makes me fall for her all over again, tugs at my arm until I lean down on my elbows over her. She spreads her legs wide underneath me and reaches down, taking my cock in her hand, and guides it into her opening. "Can I tell you a secret?" She whispers the words with a hitch in her breath while I take her again, inch by inch.

"Anything."

"I want you, too. *This* much."

CHAPTER TWENTY-SEVEN

Vivienne

I LOSE TRACK OF MY ORGASMS, LOSE TRACK OF HOW MANY TIMES we come down, bodies shaking and flooded with warmth and heat, only to start all over again. All I know is that it's nearly five o'clock when we finally emerge from Dominic's master suite, fresh out of his luxurious shower, my hair displayed in damp waves around my shoulders. I'm wearing one of his dress shirts over a pair of his boxers, the fabric giving off an expensive scent. I don't think I've ever felt so satisfied, so good, in my entire life.

Folding my legs underneath me on the sofa—I see now that it's covered in fine, soft, buttery leather, and the coolness feels delicious against my newly showered legs—I watch Dominic through the doorway into the kitchen. "Where'd you learn to do that?"

"Do what, open a bottle of wine?" He's popping the cork on a bottle, taking two glasses down from a cupboard over the sink. The curve at the corner of his mouth gives away that he likes this—he likes these moments when he's being funny. Dominic isn't wearing a shirt, just a pair of shorts, and I can't tear my eyes away from the strong lines of his shoulders, the cut of his abs rising above the kitchen counter. *Damn,* he is hot. And not just that. Not just that, but every time I think of that whispered confession—*I love you, Vivienne Davis*—my whole body goes warm and giddy.

"No...*pleasure a woman* like that."

He looks up at me, eyes sparkling, and turns to pull a plate down from another cupboard. "Years of practice."

"You didn't take some kind of class?"

He cocks his head to the side. "Oh, right. There *was* that course at Yale."

I laugh. It doesn't make me jealous that he's been with other women. Today I reaped all the benefits of his experience. After this, it's going to be hard to call to mind any of the other men I've been with—they all pale in comparison in every way.

A quiet buzzing from across the room distracts me from my Dominic-worship. The pattern sounds familiar, but—

It stops, and I watch him arrange some slices of French bread on the plate, reach for some cheese in the fridge—

The buzzing starts again. With a jolt, I realize that it's my phone, ringing in my purse by the door.

"Oh, shit," I whisper under my breath, jumping up from the couch. Then I remember myself. I don't want to look *too* panicked, but there's a hustle in my step when I cross to my purse and dig my phone out. *Please let it be Margo. Please let it be Margo.*

It's not Margo.

The number on the screen isn't saved into my contacts list, so there's no name to go with it, but I recognize the digits. Of course I do. It's my boss calling—and not Mr. Overhiser, but Milton Jeffries, my boss at the FBI.

My heart leaps into my throat, my gut going cold. Is he calling because he knows I've fucked Dominic? In his view, that would really be fucking up. Or is he calling because—

I can't wait for a voicemail, and he'll be pissed if I do, so I swipe the screen to answer the call and raise the phone to my ear. "Vivienne Davis," I say, like it's no big deal.

I cross back into the living room, giving Dominic a little wave and pointing at the phone, and then I head into the hallway toward the master suite. There's an office along that hall, and I go inside, closing the door gently behind me, and move toward the window, as far away from the door as I can get.

Not that Dominic is going to follow me to spy on my phone call. He's *not.* But this is—

"Are you at the Wilder Building?" Milton's response is clipped, strained.

"No, I—"

"Where are you?"

"I'm not far." My mind scrambles for an explanation, but I don't have one, except— "I was following a lead. I can be back there in fifteen minutes. What's going on, Milton?"

"The surveillance team caught something while sorting through the bulk emails." A few people are assigned to the case who watch every piece of email that goes in and out of Wilder Industries, trying to figure out who's responsible for the theft, but the data isn't always complete and there are massive holes to fill. "From what they can tell, there's going to be an information exchange in thirty minutes. We need you on the ground."

"Thirty minutes? But that'll be after five."

Milton makes a short sound that's meant to indicate that I'm being stupid. "All the better, Viv. At least some of the staff will have gone home by then, right? Narrow it down..."

"I know. Of course. I'll be back there shortly."

I end the call before he can ask me what lead I was following and where it had taken me that I needed to be away from the Wilder Building on a Monday afternoon.

I will my hands to stop trembling and go back out into the living room, where Dominic is setting out the plate of bread and cheese and glasses of wine on the table. The instant he sees my face, his smile disappears.

"What is it, Vivienne?"

"I—I have to go back to work."

He narrows his eyes, and then his mouth turns up into another smile. "If Overhiser is giving you a problem—"

"It's just something I need to finish. I forgot about it before I left." I grin back at him, trying to be convincing, and I can't tell if it's working. "Don't be mad at me, boss."

I can see him considering this situation, considering whether he should just tell me to stay, that *he* owns the company, that ultimately he's my boss and he'll have the final say.

I try again. "I just don't want—" I bite my lip, looking down at the floor, hating that I'm being deceptive, hating the fact that after all this, after what we had together this afternoon—*I love you, Vivienne Davis—*

"I understand." Dominic crosses behind the couch. I look up into his eyes, wondering why he's not going to press for details, wondering why—and then it hits me. He *trusts* me. We're both still in the afterglow of our time together in bed. My heart warms, then sinks, then aches at the sight of him. He leans down, taking my face in his strong hands, and kisses me softly on the lips. "Just come back when you're done, okay?"

"Okay," I whisper, wishing it was over already, wishing I could just retreat to his bedroom with him and never come out.

But instead I put my clothes back on, take the elevator downstairs, and throw myself into the Town Car he's called for me.

Back to work.

CHAPTER TWENTY-EIGHT

Dominic

If Vivienne Davis is the ocean, I'm drowning in her, and happily. The scent of her, the sight of her, the sound of her—it's the first thing on my mind when I wake up in the morning, and the last thing on my mind when I go to sleep at night, even if that sounds so sickeningly cliché it should never be said by anyone ever again.

There's a clear divide in my life now. There is the time before Monday, and then the time after Monday. Before I took her, told her I loved her, before she admitted the same to me, before I made her mine...and after.

Now she *is* mine. Now we're not dancing around the breathless attraction that surges through the air when we look at each other. We're in it, together.

Or at least, I'm in it.

Vivienne stayed with me Monday night, but she wouldn't let me drop her off in front of the building. She'd grinned at me, naked and pink, fresh from the shower. "Just because *I'm* over the fact that you're my boss, doesn't mean everyone else will be."

"Vivienne, I *own* Wilder Enterprises."

"So?" She shook her head. "I still want to...I still want my career." She'd glanced down at the floor when she said that, like it was something to be slightly ashamed of. "I don't want anyone to think I got something out of this by sleeping with my boss."

That was the first indication that, yes, we're in love, but no, Vivienne isn't going to jump into an entirely new life head first. As much as I'd like for her to move in with me right now and stay in my bed until the end of time.

She also wouldn't stay at my place *every* night.

"I love you," I'd whispered into her ear late Tuesday evening as she stood at the door to the elevator. "Stay."

Vivienne had taken in a deep breath like she had to brace herself for what she was about to say. "I *love* you, Dominic. But I just—" She'd pressed her head against my shoulder, arms wrapped around my neck. "I just want to do this the *right* way, you know?" Something in her voice made me think she wasn't quite telling me everything, but I didn't press. Vivienne is a mystery I'm learning more about every day. Acting like some controlling asshole isn't going to get me anywhere.

Even if Vivienne is the type who, behind closed doors, likes to be punished, likes to have a red ass.

I'm in the middle of a meeting the following Monday when my cock jumps in my pants. Thankfully I'm sitting at the conference room table, so it hides the tent it makes in my trousers. My mind has drifted away from the meeting topic, a rundown of some of the new energy investments we're preparing to make in Central American companies. Instead, I've been thinking about Vivienne bending over the arm of the couch on Sunday afternoon, begging for me to please, *please*—

I can't force the grin off of my face. She wants what she wants, and sometimes, like Sunday afternoon, she wants to submit to me like no woman ever has before.

"Mr. Wilder?"

"Yes. I'm listening." Childs' face is sober. *Have* I been listening? I can't remember what the last thing anyone at this meeting said, but I feel the smile vanishing from my face. "What is it, Childs?"

"I think we're going to lose this opportunity, Mr. Wilder."

I wrack my brain to figure out what the hell he's referring to. "Refresh me on why exactly." I try not to do this shit—try not to be the absent-minded owner of the company who pushes all responsibility off onto other people—and today I've obviously failed miserably.

"They're demanding another level of commitment," Childs drawls, leaning back in his seat. He's looking at me through narrowed eyes. None of them would dare challenge me about something as stupid as daydreaming during a meeting, but my heart picks up the pace. Jesus. This is *exactly* why I've stayed away from women the last few years. Vivienne is worth it, of course she is, but—

"What level of commitment would that be? You've been running point on this, haven't you?"

"Yes." Childs leans forward again, folding his hands on the desk. "Yes, but this group exerts more regional influence than we thought. They're not so much separate companies as individual entities under a pretty massive umbrella corporation, and they hold a lot of sway."

Irritation spikes in my chest. "What are you saying, Childs? Spit it out."

"They want a sit-down with you to ensure that you'll personally be overseeing the partnership."

"And then what?" The initial meeting is never the only thing. It *never* is.

Childs raises one shoulder, then lets it drop. "As far as I can tell, they'd like to host the meeting in their own offices."

My jaw goes tight. Fuck this. Fuck making a special trip to Central America just to shake hands with some second-rate businessmen and tell them that, of course, as the owner of Wilder Enterprises, I'll be wasting my time making sure every detail of the partnership with them is—

That thought stops me dead.

Wasting my time?

Not giving a shit about details of a partnership that could ultimately be worth billions?

No. *No.*

I can love Vivienne Wilder, and I do love Vivienne Wilder. I can't get enough of her. But I can't let myself go down this path. I can't let everything in my life go in favor of—

In favor of what, exactly? A relationship that could last the rest of my life?

I take in a deep breath and let it out. There has to be some kind of fucking balance here, and I'll find it. There's no doubt I'll find it. But for today, at least, I can't think about Vivienne any more. I can't let her derail a massive energy partnership that will extend Wilder Enterprises' reach through more countries than ever before. That would be damn irresponsible. That would be something my *father* would do.

Not a chance.

"What's the timeline on this?"

"We're supposed to finalize things in the second week of August, if all goes right." Childs taps his fingers against the hardwood surface of the meeting table. "I'm just...concerned that they're getting cold feet."

"I'll have Emily arrange something with your office. I assume you'll also attend."

"Of course. I'll have my girl send over everything Emily needs to start making the arrangements."

"Excellent."

I stand up abruptly. I need to get my head back on straight, and I'm hoping a break for lunch will do that. I only wish I could snuff out the cold pit of worry that's churning in my gut.

What if I can't figure out how to make this balance between Vivienne and Wilder Enterprises work?

I push the thought from my head, dismiss the meeting, and go upstairs for lunch.

CHAPTER TWENTY-NINE

Vivienne

THE MAD DASH BACK TO WILDER ENTERPRISES ENDED UP being a bust, and I'm still fuming about it a week later.

Milton had been half right. There *were* fewer people in the office than there would have been in the middle of the afternoon. What Milton *didn't* know, however, was that half the executives are attending a conference in London next week, which means that their staff members were busy working overtime to make sure every last detail was smoothed out well in advance. Overhiser *isn't* one of the executives heading to Europe, which explains why he was gone—as usual—before Dominic had a chance to sweep me off my feet.

I told a few innocuous white lies once I got back to my desk, but finalized some details for a meeting scheduled later in the week so I could point to something concrete if anyone asked. Only then did I set about snooping as best I could in plain sight with so many people still around. I made calls to other departments to ask if specific people were still there, casually following up to see if *anyone* was actually there at all.

The executive level was a hive of activity, like it tends to be before a big trip. There were a few people staying late in the marketing department, three more in tech support, a bunch of people from the janitorial staff...

I'd wanted to scream.

Instead, I printed off files and came up with excuses to visit the other floors to spy on what was happening.

It wasn't the most subtle of investigations, because—as Milton must have known when he called me—the information that was being exchanged with the Chinese wasn't going to be transferred in some obvious way, like being handed over in a black briefcase. The transaction would likely be transmitted in an email that the culprit hoped was secure, hoped was secret.

Well, at least all indications pointed to this method anyway.

That didn't stop me from keeping my eyes peeled for any kind of handoff between an employee and someone who appeared to be from the outside.

Overhiser receives a master file listing all of the meetings scheduled on a given day, same as all the executives, and when I wasn't walking the building, coming up with feasibly related questions for as many people as I could without setting off any alarm bells, I studied the schedule for anything—*anything*—seemingly out of the ordinary. Anyone visiting from a foreign country, China specifically, but anywhere outside the United States. Anyone making a delivery from a company with a generic business name or title.

Everything came up empty.

Just after six-thirty, I burst into one meeting between a marketing consultant and a representative from one of the Midwestern states, only realizing too late that my behavior looked desperate and strange, exactly the opposite of how a competent undercover FBI agent should appear.

My only saving grace was that *most* of the floors have the same layout—the only three that are different are the ones housing Dominic's private office, his penthouse on the top floor, and the executive level, which is configured so that each executive has the maximum amount of space possible for their glassed-in offices.

I had put a hand to my forehead, the blush in my cheeks entirely unmanufactured. "I'm *so* sorry, uh—" I took a quick glance at his nameplate. "Charles. I got off on the wrong floor."

He was a handsome gentleman, the marketing consultant, with blonde hair that wouldn't have looked out of place on a beach in the Hamptons. He'd laughed indulgently, looking me up and down appreciatively. "You can make that mistake any time."

I'd nodded, pretending to be in on the joke, and backed out of the room.

I left the building and called Milton from down the block. "I'm not seeing anything."

"Nothing?"

"There are—" I swallowed my frustration. "There are way more people still here than you'd think for after hours, and there's nothing drawing my attention. I've been all over the damn building." I took a deep breath. "It must have been via email, Milton, or somebody got it past me while my back was turned." I could feel his level of confidence in me fading by the moment.

"We'll watch everything outgoing from here," Milton had replied with a sigh. "Just keep looking. Anything new on your guy?"

"Not a thing." I wasn't proud to admit it, and even less proud to say the next thing that had to be said. "I might have been wrong about him."

"We're all wrong at one point or another, Viv. Just keep your nose to the grindstone."

Well, I've been keeping my nose to the grindstone every day since then, and there's not a single crack I can exploit at Wilder Enterprises. I thought Overhiser was my big break, but now he's just an irritation I have to deal with—cheerfully and professionally every single moment—while I try to find some other way to solve this case.

"Vivienne."

His quiet voice from the doorway of Overhiser's office sends a thrill of pleasure down my spine. It doesn't matter that I have been sifting through emails for the last hour, gritting my teeth and willing one of them to contain something that's worth for-warding on to the team.

"Mr. Wilder." I stand up smoothly. "What can I do for you?" Things might be going to shit as far as the case is going, but see-ing him makes my heart sing. I wish I could cross the room right now and kiss him like there's no tomorrow, but it's only five-thir-ty. There are enough people lingering around still to make that a very *bad* idea.

"Were you on your way out? I have a few things I'd like to discuss with you." He speaks in an even tone, loudly enough for anyone passing by to hear. He's covering, getting me out of here, and there's a glint in his eye that tells me the first stop on his agenda is his penthouse.

"I *was*," I say with a smile. "Just let me finish up one thing." I take thirty full seconds to sign out of my computer, clicking back out of the list of emails I've been sorting through. "I'm happy to walk out with you."

"That would be excellent."

Nothing in his voice betrays us to anyone else—anyone ex-cept me. I can see the pent-up energy he's carrying in the line of his shoulders, and I feel it in that instant—I'm wound up tight, too.

I gather my purse. I can't stay at Dominic's all night. I need to stay focused, keep working, keep fighting this. But I *can* lose myself in him for an hour or two first.

Outside, in the car, he waits until we're a block down from

Wilder Enterprises, then takes me into his arms, kissing me hard, kissing me hot, kissing me like he loves me, and as if there's nothing else he'd rather be doing in the world.

CHAPTER THIRTY

Dominic

O N WEDNESDAY AFTERNOON, THE NOTE ARRIVES.

I think it's from Vivienne at first, and my heart leaps in my chest. It would be a clever answer to the white envelopes I like to send to her desk, either alone or with gifts—although I should probably be more discreet about the gifts, now that we've reached another level in our relationship. Even if that level is still hidden from prying eyes at the moment.

This envelope doesn't have anything on it except my name in a neat print, which should be the first hint that it's not from her. Vivienne always writes in cursive, and her penmanship is distinctive.

I tear open the envelope and a notecard falls out. *Now* I recognize the block print. It's from Chris.

Things are ramping up at the Department, it reads. *We're seeing an uptick of activity—info moving from place to place. Not much longer.*

—CO

I shred the note into fifty tiny pieces and tip them all into the trash bin next to my desk. I was knee-deep in contract negotiations with a potential partner in London, but I stopped everything when the note arrived. Now I wish I hadn't.

I'm sick to death of this business with the FBI, and my jaw has clenched tight at the thought of it. I need to maintain some semblance of control over my company, and I can't do it while there's someone working for me who's stealing. I don't know what Chris thinks he's playing at.

If I hadn't promised him that I'd let them do their work, this could be resolved by now.

Well—resolved in that I'd just fire anyone who came under even a hint of suspicion and move on. That would narrow the field for the FBI.

I swivel around in my chair and look out over the five o'clock skyline of New York City. Vivienne has plans with a friend tonight, so she's ducking out as soon as she can, and I won't see her until tomorrow.

The investigation nags at my mind.

How long has this been going on? What was it that Chris said at that first meeting?

This has been going on a few weeks...

I had met him at the bar right around the time I met Vivienne.

The two thoughts collide and then repel off one another in my mind. Vivienne arrived entirely by chance. People come in and out of the Executive Support Department all the time as executives choose new staff, people move up or out, or they take their skills and transfer to other departments. It can't possibly be that—

It's hard to even formulate the thought.

It can't *possibly* be that Vivienne is involved with this.

If she *was* involved in this, it could only be in one of two ways, and I don't know which would be a bigger blow to me.

She could be the inside person. *She* could be the person who's handing off company secrets to the Chinese contact. But no—that wouldn't make any sense. According to Chris, the investigation started, and it wasn't long after that they put someone undercover on the case, someone inside the company.

But Vivienne *couldn't* be working undercover for the FBI. She would have told me. She wouldn't upend what we have on a lie like that.

I pick up a pen to keep marking up a contract, turning back to my desk, but I can't seem to formulate the letters on the page into anything readable.

The timing *was* very close. Too close. But it couldn't be. Could it?

I tap my fingers against the surface of my desk. I've never

looked up Vivienne's personnel file, but I could, and it might put my mind at ease about this whole thing if I do. Because as long as Vivienne's not involved in it, this whole thing can just be an inconvenience that will fix itself in time—whether I have to be the one to do it, or the FBI finally makes a move.

I jiggle the mouse next to my keyboard, waking up the computer. My login allows me access to everything there is to access on the Wilder Enterprises server. I rarely do this, so at first the filing system seems like a damn maze. I need to have someone from tech support come up here and refresh my memory. I don't like having a weakness like that.

A few frustrating minutes later, I've finally located the personnel files for employees who hired on in the last three months. I scroll down, down...and there she is.

I hesitate, my mouse poised to click on the file to open it.

We might have an unspoken agreement that Vivienne likes some kink in the bedroom, that sometimes she wants to lose herself in a little bit of submission, but I have no doubt that this would be crossing the line in her mind. Not that the lines aren't already blurred—they are, just because she works here and I own the company. What we've been doing already puts us in uncertain territory.

This is about protecting yourself. Once I have the thought, I can't push it away. Have I really spent all these years building incredible wealth only to jeopardize it by falling for someone who's just playing a role?

My father comes to mind, living on a decent property in up-state New York, largely because of my own generosity. Even so, I don't see him. We don't speak. He's not proud of what he did, and neither am I. It's the elephant in the room any time we're together, so we avoid that by never being together.

I don't want that type of life for myself.

I open the file.

It starts with all the standard information—her staff ID picture, her name, her birthdate, her current address. The address matches up with the place I've dropped her off. No red flags there, and the sight of her face smiling out at me from the computer makes my heart thump hard against my ribs.

I scroll down through the file. She interviewed with someone in Human Resources—I don't recognize the name—and they left glowing notes about how her personality is an excellent fit for the open position in Executive Support. Even her resume seems to be neatly in order, if a little sparse. I'd have expected someone like Vivienne to have more meat there, and I narrow my eyes at the document. *This* got through the HR system when she applied? I wonder if she knows someone in *that* department. She's never mentioned it, but...

I scroll down again. *Recommended for this position by Georgina Lillianfield.*

Now that—*that* seems out of character. From what I've heard from the executives, Ms. Lillianfield is wickedly efficient, but not the kind to gush.

How does Vivienne know her?

My stomach lurches, and I abruptly click out of the file.

What the hell am I *doing*?

I *trust* Vivienne. I *love* her. If she knows Lillianfield, then she knows her. This isn't the kind of thing to throw everything we have away over.

I push all of it out of my mind, pull out my phone, and send her a message.

Tell me I can see you tonight.

A few minutes later, she replies.

Only if I can see you first. :)

My heart settles down.

If only I could say the same for the creeping doubt in the back of my mind.

CHAPTER THIRTY-ONE

Vivienne

THIS INVESTIGATION IS GETTING INTO MY HEAD, UNDER MY skin, and I have to do something about it. I have to do something to release some of the tension before I grind my teeth into oblivion all night.

Dominic wants to see me, and it's a damn good thing, because I *need* him.

I need him to take control for an hour or two. I need him to reduce me to a bundle of lust-soaked nerves, because when I come out on the other side, my mind will be settled, my mind will be at ease, and then *maybe* I can figure out what the hell is knotted at the center of this theft. It should be easy. It should be open and shut. This was going to be my big moment of triumph, my big break, but—

I follow Dominic into the lobby of his penthouse. The moment I cross the threshold, my shoulders relax in spite of the thoughts rattling around in my brain, and I hear him let out a big breath like he's been holding it in all afternoon. We were both quiet in the car, watching the blocks roll by, but now we're here, and I'm so, *so* ready.

He wraps his arms around me from behind, pulling me in close, nuzzling his chin into the side of my neck, and all of me melts into him.

"It's been a long day," he murmurs in my ear.

I twist in his grasp, putting my arms around his neck. "Are you too tired? Do you want to lie down for a while?"

A wicked look comes into his eyes. "Lie down with you?" He drops his voice just a touch, and I know there's going to be no rest until he's thoroughly finished with me.

Just how I want it.

He leans down slowly, edging toward me, his hands tightening around my waist, and I breathe in his clean, manly scent. The core of me goes hot, my pussy is wet already, and I wonder why we didn't get started in the car.

It doesn't matter. We're here now.

His lips make the softest, gentlest contact, like we're kissing for the very first time, and it makes me tilt back in his arms, groaning out loud. "Dominic—"

"What?" He pulls back, eyes dancing.

"Don't tease me." I meant to say it in a haughty tone, but instead it comes out as more of a plea. "I'm—"

He pulls me back into him, and I feel his erection pressing against my hips. "You need something more."

"Yes..."

"You need something harder."

"I—" My throat goes tight with just how *much* I need it. I've never thought of myself as the kind of woman who needs a man to take her in hand in the bedroom, but right now, with the pressure of my job bearing down on me, the fact that I can't share it all with Dominic, I have to have it. I have to have *him.*

He turns me in his arms, pinning my hands behind my back with one of his, and he reaches around, roughly taking my breast in his other. I arch back against him, my head thrown back against his shoulder. Through the fabric of my dress, he pinches at my nipple, sending a spike of pain and pleasure down the line from my navel to my pussy.

He doesn't ask me what I want another time. He doesn't ask what I need. He just growls into my ear, "Be a good girl." The part of my mind that's obsessed with the investigation shuts down, and all I can do is hear his voice, respond to his orders with an increasingly wet pussy and a trembling core. "Bedroom. Now."

He releases me, and I lead him to the bedroom. "Strip."

I do.

Then he gestures toward a large ottoman in front of his

fireplace. "All fours, ass high." The air is cool between my legs, and a trickle of wetness runs down the inside of my thighs. While Dominic strips off his jacket, shirt, and tie, I go to the ottoman, only hesitating a fraction of an instant before I kneel on it, bending down into exactly the position he's asking for, private spaces exposed, breasts down on the smooth fabric, holding tight to the edges.

He runs a hand down my back, the other gliding between my spread legs, and I open up for him a little more as his fingers dance on my wet folds and slide inside.

"Mhmm," he says, his voice a low rumble. "You're ready." He dips three fingers in and I take in a breath, sighing it out. Oh, God, I need this.

Dominic strokes and rubs, circling my clit with his fingertips, until I'm a trembling puddle on the ottoman. Then, a gentle pressure on the small of my back, and his other hand slides up, spreading my ass.

My entire body tenses. "Dominic—"

"Are you mine?"

My heart is pounding. "Yes..."

"Do you trust me?"

"Yes..." This second one comes out as a whisper.

"Then relax for me, sweet thing."

I force myself to relax as he spreads me again, slowly, taking his time, and then drags the pad of one finger down from the cleft in my cheeks, down one agonizing inch at a time, down and down, until he presses it firmly against my crinkled hole. I'm flooded with shame, but more than that, I'm swimming in desire.

"Relax."

Dominic removes the finger and sucks it into his mouth, then replaces it against my hole. "Relax..." He repeats, and then he increases the pressure, working his finger against my resistance until finally it pops in.

I cry out, and he presses his hand against my lower back again. "How does it feel, sweet thing?"

"It—I'm so embarrassed."

"Don't be." He works his finger in and out, pressing it a little deeper with every movement. It feels thick, it feels *big,* but it doesn't necessarily feel bad, even though my face is scarlet and my knuckles are white where they're clenching the sides of the ottoman. Dominic works until it's all the way in. "Good girl."

A gush of wetness gives me away, and he lets out a short laugh.

"Don't move."

I hold as still as I can while he crosses the room. A drawer opens, then closes, and the next sensation to wash over me is a cool liquid against my hole.

"Oh—"

"*Relax.*" This time, his voice is as commanding as it's ever been, and I press my lips together and obey.

Then there's something thicker than his fingers at my hole, and his hand is on my back.

"You're mine," he says, and then he presses it in, presses it slowly, presses it absolutely relentlessly. I have no choice but to open for it, to let it in, and I don't recognize the sounds I'm making. "Good girl," he says, pushing it in a final inch, and I feel my asshole close around a narrower section of it.

"Oh, God, it's *huge*."

He leans down, threading his fingers through my hair, and turns my face to him. His eyes are fiery, piercing, and then his mouth is on mine, he's pulling me up and away from the ottoman, carrying me to the bed. Spreading me out. Thrusting inside me. I suck in a breath of him, bite down on his shoulder, wrap my legs around him—and I'm gone, lost in a crashing wave of desire and release, all the worry erased from my mind.

CHAPTER THIRTY-TWO

Dominic

I SHOULD BE OVER THE DAMN MOON.

I should be beside myself with satisfaction, with joy, because last week with Vivienne was amazing. Beyond amazing—it was on a plane I never thought I'd witness with any woman. An absolutely intoxicating mix of submission and freedom, and all of it seamless, all of it transitioning without a hitch.

Vivienne is so open with me in those moments, so vulnerable about what she wants from me, what she needs from me, and it's like we don't even have to speak to understand each other.

But when I woke up this morning, all the calm was gone.

What if there's some other...*motive* for being so open?

The reality is that I have to focus on work. Vivienne and I

have our evenings, have our nights, but while I'm at the Wilder Building my attention needs to be here one hundred percent.

"Mr. Wilder, everything's in place for the meeting." Emily stands in my doorway with a leather folio in her hands, the last item I'll need to take with me into the conference room.

"Thanks, Emily. I'll be right there."

It's the first meeting of the day, and already I can feel my mind wandering off into places it's definitely *not* supposed to be. But there's no other alternative. I square my shoulders, slide my phone into my pocket, and go.

* * *

It's almost four o'clock by the time I'm able to exhale all the jittery energy that's followed me around all day. I wonder what the hell Chris O'Connor and his team are doing right now. I wonder who the undercover agent is. I want to go stalk the floors until I find him, but how will I be able to tell?

I bend my head over a sheaf of contracts waiting for my signature.

Stop thinking about this shit.

A gentle knock at my door makes my jaw clench with irritation. How the fuck am I supposed to get this done if I'm interrupted every five seconds? I look up, ready to dismiss whoever it is with a cutting remark, but I can't.

Because it's Vivienne.

Her face is a little pink, like she's been thinking of what we did last night and getting ashamed in retrospect, but her smile makes me smile back. "Ms. Davis."

"Mr. Wilder—could I come in for a minute?"

"Of course. What do you need?"

Behind her back, I see Emily move down the hallway and get on the elevator. She's undoubtedly going down to the seventh floor, where Wilder Enterprises maintains a state-of-the-art copy center. If you wanted, you could bind an entire book down there and sell it on the street outside.

But book binding is the last thing on my mind.

Vivienne steps up to the edge of my desk and looks down at a folder in her hands.

"Do you have something for me, Ms. Davis?"

When she looks up again, her eyes are sparkling. "It's a decoy." She opens the folder and shows me that it's empty. "I thought— listen, maybe this is a stupid idea. I'm regretting coming up here more than a little right now."

"Tell me." My heart aches when I see her, aches and grows warm and beats hard, and right now is no exception. The warring thoughts are taking place only in my mind. I should get back to work. Vivienne should get back to work. We should save this for later.

"I thought we could...go on a date."

I look at her with narrowed eyes. "A date?"

"Yes. A date to somewhere we've never been before."

I look past her once more to see if Emily has returned. She hasn't. "We could go Saturday."

"What about right now?" She's smiling tentatively, but with every moment the conversation lengthens, the smile gets dimmer. "I thought I could tempt you outside for the last hour of the day. I wanted to...return the favor from last week."

"Last week?"

The smile flickers. "You took me home with you on a Monday afternoon, a little before the day was *officially* over. I thought..." Her voice lowers, and two bright spots of color appear on her cheeks. "You know what, this was a mistake." She wrinkles her nose. "A mistake. Let's do something on the weekend. It's only two days away." She clears her throat, glances over her shoulder. "Thank you, Mr. Wilder," she says in a voice meant to carry, and then she turns away, toward the door.

I'm out of my seat in an instant, my entire chest aching, and I catch her by the wrist. I lower my own voice. "Do you know something, Vivienne Davis?"

"What?" Her eyes are wide and searching, but her body is still half-turned toward the door, like she can't wait to get out of here.

"I love you."

The smile comes back to her face, wide and pure. "I love *you*."

"I'm just—I had a lot to do today."

"The weekend," she says again, sounding calm and assured. "The weekend will be fine. I don't know what I was thinking." Then she laughs. "I guess I wasn't thinking."

"No. We'll go now."

"Dominic, we don't have to—"

"Be waiting for me in the Town Car in five minutes."

Vivienne's eyes sparkle. "I'll be there."

She hustles out of my office and back to the elevators.

I take a deep breath in and stifle a wave of paranoia.

Get ahold of yourself, Wilder.

This isn't some crazy ploy to get me away from the office, to destabilize Wilder Enterprises. *That's* coming from someone else, someone who wants to benefit the Chinese government and betray the confidences of my company. It has nothing to do with Vivienne, and neither does the fact that I need to concentrate on my work.

Just this once, I can give in to her. Just this once, I can take an hour off in the afternoon and be with my gorgeous girlfriend.

Girlfriend.

The word, even as a thought, makes my chest feel light at the same time that a cold knot forms in my stomach. At some point, we're going to have to—

No. I'm not going to get into all that now. Yes, at some point we'll have to make some decisions about what this means for her job, for my company, but we can get to those later. For now, all I have to do is love her.

And I love her. I love her more than anything. Even Wilder Enterprises.

I repeat it to myself as I leave a note for Emily, close the door behind me, and go to meet Vivienne, my mind still behind my desk.

CHAPTER THIRTY-THREE

Vivienne

IT'S A BAD IDEA, AND I KNEW IT THE MOMENT I SAW DOMINIC'S face. And for some reason, like an idiot, I kept pressing the idea until it was crystal clear that he does *not* want to be out on some spur-of-the-moment date with me during business hours. I can't stop thinking about it, a week later.

It's a strange position to be in, because last week was a real breakthrough for me—for both of us. It's not conventional, what we have, and I know that it isn't. It's not conventional on many levels, beginning with the fact that he's my boss and ending with the fact that I'm not *really* his employee, and sooner or later it's a house of cards that's going to come crashing down.

But in his arms last night, I felt none of that—and maybe it was a mistake to let it go.

Maybe it was a mistake to think I could separate the two things, keep a wall between them that would let me do my job while also letting me fall in love.

Because I *have* fallen in love. I've spoken the words out loud. I can't even think of Dominic without thinking of how he makes me feel, how secure, how steady.

Except today.

Today, the look on his face makes me feel like I'm on a ship but I haven't gotten my sea legs and I might never get them at all. There's a strange energy between us.

I haven't slept well lately. Maybe that's what it is.

When he climbs into the Town Car next to me, I do my best to pretend that everything is fine, and Dominic grins at me. I'm careful not to notice the strain in his eyes—for a moment. But when Craig pulls the car away from the curb, I can't help myself.

"Dominic, are you all right?"

He looks into my eyes, taking my hand in his. "I'm fine. A long day, that's all."

"You know—" It seems so damn disingenuous to say this to him when I can't breathe a word of what's causing *me* stress. "You can talk to me, if something is going on. I won't say anything at work, if you're worried that—"

He raises my hand to his lips and kisses my knuckles. "I'm not worried about you spilling company secrets."

My heart leaps into my throat. It's such a random choice of words.

The blood is draining from my face, and it's going to be a damn disaster if I can't get myself under control *right this second.*

I force a laugh, and it sounds genuine enough. "I'm not digging around for *secrets,* Mr. Wilder. I meant that I wouldn't reveal how you feel to anyone at the office."

He gazes into my eyes, the corners of his own crinkled. "What if how I feel is the most *valuable* company secret?"

I nod solemnly. "I'll never tell."

He kisses my cheek, then wraps one arm around me, pulling me in close as Craig steers us through the traffic. "Why don't you tell me where we're going? I'm assuming you've conspired with my driver on this."

"Only a little. But I'm not telling."

He teases me, and I tease him back, and the words fall like raindrops around me, barely making an impression. Can he feel my heart beating hard against my rib cage? Can he sense the way my throat keeps going tight when I remember his words?

Does Dominic *know?*

No. I tell it to myself over and over again, like a silent prayer. Dominic doesn't know. He made a joke about corporate secrets, and that's all that was.

Craig pulls into Central Park, and Dominic straightens up. "You've never been to Central Park before?" He looks at me skeptically, and this time, my laugh is a real one.

"I've been to Central Park. There's someplace inside it I've never been to."

"What kind of place?"

"You'll see."

We step out of the car into the blinding summer heat, and I frown. Dominic takes a big breath and strips off his coat, tossing it back into the car. He leans in. "Be ready for us, Craig." Craig nods and pulls away, probably to park somewhere in the shade.

Dominic rolls up his sleeves, and I raise a hand to my eyes to shade them from the harsh sun. "Where are we going?"

"It's not far. You can hear it from here."

There's carnival music wafting through the air toward us, faint at first, and getting stronger while we walk through the park, every step on the sidewalk taking us closer to the skating rink. My hands feel shaky—this is seeming like a bigger and bigger risk with every moment that goes by—and I glance up at Dominic. His forehead is wrinkled, but he's clearly trying his best not to look confused.

When the rink comes into view, his face cracks into a smile. "An amusement park?"

"I read—" I swallow down my nervousness. I don't know what the hell I was thinking, planning this little outing. I just wanted a little more normalcy squeezed into my day, a little less of the prickling anxiety that's filling more of my hours every day that I can't make headway on this investigation. "I read online that they turn the skating rink into an amusement park in the summer so that they can use the space all year round instead of just leaving it empty."

Dominic is grinning at me.

"I thought we could enjoy ourselves for an hour or two and just—what?"

"You know, there are other ways to enjoy ourselves that don't involve dying of heat stroke."

We're nearing the booth at the entrance of the little amusement park—Victoria Gardens—and I slip a bill out of my purse, ready to pay the attendant. "They have ice cream inside. I'll even buy you a soda, if you want."

I pay the woman sitting on a tall stool behind the bench and pull Dominic forward. He laughs, shaking his head. A billionaire and an undercover FBI agent, visiting an amusement park full of ridiculous attractions and rides, vendors selling pink and blue puffs of cotton candy and balloons, all of it soaked in the late afternoon heat.

"I'm going to take you up on that," he promises, squeezing my hand, and my heart resumes its regular rhythm.

Everything is okay, I tell myself firmly.

And I almost believe it.

But just at the last moment, I look across at Dominic one more time. He's looking at me, eyes serious and hard, like he's trying to make a decision. I smile, and the expression is gone in a flash, but I see it.

"Do you know what?" I have to break the silence. I have to. The cold anxiety glides down the back of my neck.

"What, Vivienne Davis?"

"I love cotton candy. Let's get some."

The sweetness doesn't cover my fear.

CHAPTER THIRTY-FOUR

Dominic

WE STAY AT THE AMUSEMENT PARK FOR TWO HOURS, careening between the kind of innocent good time I haven't had since I was a child and a taut tension that I can't quite explain.

No. I *can* explain it, and that's what's putting me on edge.

I don't know what made me bring up company secrets. I wasn't planning to interrogate Vivienne about why she *really* applied for the job at Wilder Enterprises. I was planning to be over it, over it completely, and to continue on with my life until we're forced to make an actual decision about us.

But I felt how her body froze when I said it.

I did feel it. I'm not making it up. I wasn't imagining it—at least, I don't *think* I was.

It's so damn hard to tell.

My stomach goes tight with the indecision rotting my core.

I felt her tense up, but I saw her laugh without hesitation. I saw her pick up the thread of the conversation like she had no idea what I might be talking about, like there's no feasible reason on earth why she would *ever* steal company secrets.

There are times at the amusement park that seem completely sublime, like when she licks a stray drop of ice cream off of my chin in full view of everyone, in public, laughing at the sweetness, her dark hair pulled up in a clip at the back of her head. Or when she leans into me as we move through the crowd, heat be damned, and I run my hand down her back, feeling the light dampness from the humidity at the small of her back. Or when she sighs, slipping her hand into mine, and smiles up at me.

But there are also moments when I don't know who I'm looking at, when I can't be sure that the person in front of me is really who she says she is at all.

I need to get my head in order, and make a decision about this, because it's eating me alive. More than once, I catch her staring at me, brow furrowed, a frown turning the corners of her lips downward. When she sees me looking, she smiles again, and I think—*what if she's just worried that I'm not enjoying myself? What if it's as simple as that?*

It could be as simple as that.

It could be.

We tumble into the back of the Town Car exhausted from

the heat, and Craig glances into the rearview mirror. "Did you two kids have fun?"

"Enough fun to last a hundred years," Vivienne says, kicking off her heels. "Why didn't I wear more sensible shoes?"

"Why didn't you plan a more sensible outing?" I tease, leaning in to kiss the side of her neck below her jaw and tasting the fine salt that's collected there.

"I didn't want a sensible outing," she cries, leaning back into the seat while Craig pulls into traffic. "Everyone always wants a sensible outing." Then she shakes her head. "Things that aren't sensible have been happening for a while now. Why not make them fun?"

"What do you mean?"

I reach over to the dial that controls the temperature and up the air conditioning several levels.

Vivienne considers me from across the seat. "Well, for one, I met *you*. It's hardly sensible to run into a billionaire on the sidewalk carrying an oversized box of doughnuts and then end up..."

Her voice trails off, but a blush rises to her cheeks.

"Why the doughnuts, anyway?" That rainstorm day seems like a thousand years ago and yesterday all at the same time.

"I wanted to—" She makes a face, looks out the window. "I wanted people in the department to like me."

"And you thought you'd bribe them with doughnuts?"

Vivienne shrugs. "It's worked before."

"Oh? Where at?"

She looks back at me, smiling with closed lips. "Wilder Enterprises isn't my first job, you know."

"I can't imagine that it would be. You're far too—" I give her a cocky look.

"Are you about to call me *old*, Dominic Wilder?" She drops her mouth open in faux outrage.

"No. You're far too delicious to be old. But even if you were—" I lean in for another kiss. She tastes like cotton candy somehow, still. "I'd still want you."

Vivienne pushes me away playfully. "Don't be vulgar."

"Age isn't vulgar."

"Let's not go down that road," she laughs.

"Okay. Where did you work before this, then? Tell me which companies in town are so easily swayed by a beautiful woman with doughnuts to pass around."

I don't know why I'm pushing her like this. I don't know what I'm hoping to get out of this, other than some inkling of proof that she has nothing to do with this absurd FBI investigation, that she's not holding out on me, that I haven't loosened my grip on the business that's been my pride and joy for years only for someone who—

She rolls her eyes. "I worked at a publishing company for about a year. The other women in my department *loved* sweets, but especially the managing editor. She was the one who gave out assignments, and after that I always got the best one."

I nod. Was there a publishing house on her resume?

No. I'm not going to do this. I'm not going to fact-check her. I'm not going to try to catch her in a lie.

"Women are the hardest to please, I've found."

Vivienne gives me a sly grin. "Well, men are easy in comparison." Craig pulls the car up to the curb in front of her place. She pulls her purse from the floor, then slides over to kiss me, slow and deep. When we break the kiss, she breathes in. "See? I got you to take an afternoon off, and it took hardly any convincing at all."

"Why would you need me to take an afternoon off?" The suspicion has reared its ugly head again, and right away I wish I could shove the words back in my mouth, soften the tone. Vivienne's face falls.

"I didn't—" She presses her lips together. 'I just thought it would be a nice—"

My head is throbbing from being in the sun, and my gut is churning from the sweets, and I have no patience, and I feel savage and raw. "That's a fine thought, Vivienne, but next time you get one of these ideas, ask me first if it's a *nice idea* to disrupt my work because you feel like it." The words tumble out one after the other. I can't stop them.

She sucks in a sharp breath, and her chin quivers.

"Goodbye, Dominic."

Then she's out of the car, closing the door behind her. Gone.

CHAPTER THIRTY-FIVE

Vivienne

I'M JUST GOING TO GIVE HIM SOME TIME TO COOL OFF.

I'm going to give *me* some time to focus on what should be my top priority right now—getting something worthwhile out of this investigation. On Tuesday, I keep my head down, getting through the things Mr. Overhiser needs in record time so I can follow up on the emails I've been watching.

There has to be something I've missed with Overhiser. He's got so many damn shady habits—leaving early all the time, the secret club that he uses his work account to charge his membership to, all of it—but I can't connect any of them. I dedicate part of the afternoon, while I'm out personally picking up his lunch to ensure they've got the order right, trying to talk my way into said exclusive club. The doorman tells me nothing useful, and I go back to the office defeated.

Over and over again, I line up the facts that I know in my mind.

Someone is selling Wilder Enterprises' energy tech information to a contact in China.

The contact may or may not be affiliated with the Chinese government.

Whoever it was, was at Wilder Enterprises last Monday evening.

I sigh and decide to start from scratch.

I need a list of everyone who was at Wilder Enterprises last Monday evening, starting at four o'clock. It takes a little doing, but I come up with a story about how Mr. Overhiser has been tasked with some outlay oversight and needs to know, on average, how many people stay to work after hours. It's innocent enough that I half forget the story even after I've told it several times, but one by one, the emails come in, and as they do, I put together a list.

It doesn't help at all.

I feel like beating my head against the desk.

Instead, I go back to reviewing emails. The team at headquarters sent me a new flash drive that runs a secure program on my own computer so I can get more done during the work day, and I keep it open almost all day Friday, trying to get something, anything, out of it.

It's after five o'clock, almost time for me to snatch my purse out of my desk and get the hell out of here, when I find it.

The emails from the tech department are by far the most numerous, and they're mostly indecipherable messages interspersed with pieces of data that only someone with a technology fetish could even begin to understand. It makes for mind-numbing reading. Worst of all, they outsource some of their processing tasks to vendors off-site, and some of those are in foreign countries.

So far, the countries I've managed to identify are almost entirely unrelated, although there's something to be said for relaying data through a third party. Headquarters doesn't think that's what's happening. Based on the way the information is being *used,* they're fairly sure it's a direct handoff. Otherwise, we'd see similarities popping up along the chain.

Then, at the end of another similarly boring email, a single word catches my eye.

Beijing.

"Are you heading home for the night, Viv?"

It's Stephanie, one of the other chief executive assistants, poking her head in through the office door. She has her purse slung over her shoulder and a new coat of lipstick on. I glance back at my screen. It's almost five-thirty.

"The time got away from me," I say with a laugh, and switch off my screen. "Thanks for the warning—I might have sat here all night!"

"What a waste of a day!" She gives me a little wave and heads for the elevators.

I switch the screen back on, carefully to eject the flash drive properly, and drop it into my purse.

On the street outside, I wave down a cab and tell him to get to my apartment as fast as he can.

I have work to do.

* * *

Back at my apartment, I throw on a pair of shorts and a tank top and park myself on the couch with my laptop. I'm going to figure this out. My heart beats fast. This is a break, and I know it, and all I have to do is figure it out.

I keep searching through the emails from the tech department. They don't always come from the same address, but they have some features in common. I start scribbling them down on a stray notepad that was shoved down in the bottom of my purse. Then I jot down things I'm going to need to check out to make this stick. It might be common for people in that department to use different addresses for outside vendors—I don't know. I don't even know how many people work there.

My mind is humming with it, buzzing with it, and I'm almost there. I can feel it. I just need—

The knock at the door jolts me out of my flow.

I stop typing and hold my breath. There are no windows near

my apartment door, so if I just pretend that I'm not here, they'll leave me alone.

The knock comes again. "Vivienne?"

All the irritation I've been swallowing down all day rushes up from my chest, and I slap the cover of the laptop down and toss it a little too harshly, along with the notepad, onto my coffee table. Dominic was having a bad day yesterday, and he was an ass, and for once in my life, I just want to focus on my *job,* for once I just want to be left alone.

It has nothing to do with the ache in my heart from the harsh tone he used with me.

I yank open the doorway and glare up at him. He's clearly come straight from the office. "What is it?"

He looks at me, eyes wide. "I'm sorry if you're having a bad day."

"My day is fine. Yesterday *wasn't* so fine." I take in a deep breath, trying to steady myself. "I don't want to talk about this now, Dominic. I have work to do."

Shit. I didn't mean to say that—I *definitely* didn't mean to say that.

"We can talk tomorrow." I start to close the door, but he puts his hand up against it.

"You have work? That's why you can't talk to me?"

"I don't *want* to talk to you. That's the main idea."

"Do you have a second job?"

Jesus. "No."

"Then talk to me, Vivienne. I'm sorry for what I said yesterday. It was out of line, and I shouldn't have taken out my heat stroke on you."

He's trying to be funny, and I'm not in the mood. "*Tomorrow*, Dominic."

He presses his lips into a thin line. "*Now*, Vivienne."

"I'm busy."

"Doing what? There's no way you have work from Overhiser. Not tonight. He's been checked out for hours."

"I've taken on a couple of side jobs." The lie is stupid, pointless, but I'm angry and I want him to leave.

"What side jobs?"

"I don't have to tell you that."

"What the hell, Vivienne?" His frustration is boiling over. "You're lying to me."

Right then, I have a choice.

And I choose to double down.

CHAPTER THIRTY-SIX

Dominic

VIVIENNE STANDS UP TALL, FIRE FLAMING IN HER GREEN EYES, her jaw set tight. "I'm not *lying* to you."

"Is it that you're pissed at me over one thing I said, or do you actually have some other job that you've not mentioned—*at any point*—since we started seeing each other?"

"Can't it be both?"

I step into her apartment, and she backs up only enough to let me through the door. This isn't the kind of argument that should be had in the middle of the hallway. Still, she's not going to invite me in—that much is clear.

"I don't know why you won't tell me the truth."

"I *did* tell you the truth. I don't want to talk to you, and I have work to do, and you're interrupting it."

"You can't take a break for five minutes so I can apologize to you?"

"You've done that. Now you can leave." Her hands are trembling. I'm torn between wanting to wrap her in my arms and turn around and walk back out the door.

I look over her shoulder. Whatever work she's been doing has clearly been on the laptop that's shoved onto the coffee table.

I take a deep breath and try to lower my voice. "We've talked about everything for the past few weeks." I'm trying to appeal to the fact that a week ago she trusted me to take her past what I know was a sensitive boundary for her. "You *trust* me, Vivienne."

She crosses her arms over her chest, but she can't help leaning toward me, just slightly.

"Just tell me the truth."

Those are the wrong words to say. Vivienne's jaw clenches. "I'm not doing this."

"You're definitely not having a productive conversation with me, no."

"How many times do I have to say it?" Now her voice is the one spiraling out of control. "*I don't want to talk to you right now.*"

I should just let this go. I should throw my hands up and walk out of here, and I should try again when she's in the mood to talk, when she's not busy *working*—on whatever the hell work that she could possibly have.

But what she's saying just rings so damn *false.* It's Tuesday night, and Overhiser has been gone for hours. The man leaves as early as humanly possible, so there's plenty of time in the afternoon to finish everything for the rest of the week. It's not like I have experience being a chief executive assistant, but Vivienne hasn't been secretive about the fact that her boss leaves early in the afternoon.

I just want to know the truth.

And my heart is pounding, so hard it feels like it might leap out of my chest.

And it's been a long damn day, a long week, a long time since I had a fucking vacation, and that's my fault, but all of it is boiling up, boiling over. I just want a moment of real honesty with her that I can point to and say that that was when I knew—that was when I knew for sure—that she wasn't part of any of the bullshit that's been going on.

"What's your other job, Vivienne?"

She breathes in hard through her nose. "I'm. Done."

"Done with what?"

"This." She snaps her hand between us. "If you can't respect what I want, if you can't—"

"What *you* want? I'm asking a simple question. It's frankly more than a little strange that someone would come home in the middle of the week and pick up more work. And I'd get that, except you wanted an afternoon off just *yesterday* to drag me to some children's amusement park."

I'm out of control, and there's no going back. I can tell that the words are hurting her, have wounded her in a way that maybe I didn't anticipate. And since I'm already over the cliff—

"You're lying to me, Vivienne, you're lying about something, and I'm not going to have it. I'm not going to let you take my focus off what really matters if you're not going to be honest with me."

"What *really* matters?" She spits the words, but her voice is only just above a whisper. "What really matters, like your *business*? Like your *money*?" Her mouth twists in disgust. "You're like all the rest of them, Dominic."

It's a body blow, and she knows it, knows it from the glancing conversations we've had about my dad, about my mom, about the fact that I built his business back up into something from the scraps he left for me to pick up—these conversations that have never gone very far because the sore spots are still too fucking raw.

"You're right."

The words coming out of my mouth surprise even me, and Vivienne's lips part, her forehead furrowing. "What—"

"You're right." Another surge of anger, another tidal wave crashing over me. "I'm just like all the rest of the rich men you've been dating all this time—" Dripping with sarcasm, I'm dripping in rage. "—and you're just like all the women I've dated, scrabbling for a man's money because they don't want to make it for themselves. You're right." I raise both hands in the air in a cruel parody of surrender. "You're right, and I'm wrong, and you know what, Vivienne Davis? We're done. We're over."

I turn my back on her and she sucks in a pained breath. My hand is on the doorknob, my chest is exploding with my rage, and I turn back. "I'm not going to fire you," I spit at her. "I'm not going to fire you—just so we're clear—because I don't need a lawsuit and some media frenzy from the kind of woman you are. So keep your job. That's all you're going to have from me from now until the end of time."

Then I'm stalking down the hallway, jaw clenched so tight I'm not sure I'll ever be able to open my mouth again, not sure that I'll ever want to. I'm in the elevator when my phone rings in my pocket.

"What?"

"Dominic—"

Her voice sounds panicked, sounds stretched to its breaking point, but I can't. I can't right now. Maybe not ever.

"No, Vivienne. I'm done. *We're* done."

I hang up the phone.

I take in a breath.

I let it back out.

I'm done.

CHAPTER THIRTY-SEVEN

Vivienne

I TOSS MY PHONE ONTO THE COUCH AND IT BOUNCES OFF THE cushions and onto a piece of hardwood flooring not covered by the rug. I didn't throw it particularly hard, but when it makes contact, there's a *crack* that makes my heart sink even farther down past my toes.

"Shit." I run my hands through my hair and leap toward it. It's way too late. I kneel at the edge of the area rug in my living room and pick it up. The glass screen is shattered. My knees in the carpet, the cracks in the screen spider-webbing out from near the corner—*kneeling in Dominic's apartment, sheer joy on his face, my career like a broken fucking phone*—pushes me over the edge from a bizarre panicked calm to a sobbing mess.

The first heaving cry takes me by surprise, but not the rest of them. My heart is shattered, too, and the ache in my chest is so strong. *Am I having a heart attack?*

No. This is just a bad breakup.

It's the *worst* kind of breakup, because we were working in secrecy and now I can't tell anyone about it. I can't even tell Margo, because I never told Margo I was sleeping with the billionaire who owns the company which I'm working undercover at in the first place.

I laugh bitterly through a sob. How would I even explain that to another person? *He's my boss, but that's not the real problem, because he's not really my boss—*

The howl that rises in my chest is so dramatic, so over the top, that I stifle it with both hands as another arc of pain singes from my ribs to my toes.

Then I stand up, leaving the broken phone on the carpet.

I take a deep breath.

The first ten deep breaths fail to have any effect whatsoever, but I keep at it, doggedly, determinedly, for what has to be twenty minutes before I can stop sobbing.

Get a hold of yourself, Vivienne.

I say it over and over in my mind, and finally am reduced to saying it out loud until I've swallowed enough sobs that they're held at bay in my chest, a heavy point just below my sternum, and not pouring out of my mouth.

Okay.

Okay.

One more breath, and I take a seat on the couch and run through what I know. I've been doing a lot of that lately, and it hasn't seemed to help, but maybe the millionth time is the charm.

Dominic knows more than he's letting on.

He knows—now, thanks to me—that I have some kind of second job apart from Wilder Enterprises.

Dominic is done with me.

The tears threaten to come again—another failed exercise. No matter what I do, I can't think of a way through this, or out of it, without coming clean to Dominic.

And I can't come clean to him about what my job *is* without blowing the cover on the whole investigation. Even if I thought I could trust him with the information, if word *ever* got out that I compromised myself to someone who's directly involved like he is, I'd never work undercover again. My career would effectively be over.

But he knows something is up, and that's the ballgame. A man like Dominic isn't going to stay around to be played. I'm sure other women in his life have done the same thing.

Which is probably why there haven't *been* many other women, from what I understand, because weighed against what's really important…

This is pointless, and I get up from the couch again, frustrated at my own inability to get out of this spiral of thought.

I pick up the phone from the floor. The screen might be

cracked, but it still works, in its way. The first person I dial is Milton Jeffries, clearing my throat as the call connects.

"Do you have an update?"

"I broke my phone. Can you have someone from the department courier a new one over?"

Milton sighs. "That's all?"

"I'm on the verge of a break, Milton. Just give me a little more time."

"Sending someone now."

At least he doesn't feel like chatting. My voice hitched on the word *break,* and if we go on much longer, I'll be forced to say some phrase like *Wilder Enterprises* and that would make me look like *such* a strong and capable employee if I broke down crying on the phone to my boss.

No.

I lift my chin, sitting down in front of the computer again, opening the screen.

Where was I?

My throat aches with the effort of holding all of this in, but the fact of the matter—*the fact of the matter,* I say to myself in my harshest internal tone—is that I want my career to be incredible, and I don't need to be with Dominic Wilder to do it. In fact, it would be best for both of us if I was without him.

This scene didn't play out how I wanted, but in a way, it's for the best. His attention can be where it needs to be, and *my* attention can be focused on tracking down the person who's trying to undermine him.

"I wish him the best. I really do," I say out loud in my empty apartment, like I'm trying to convince Margo that this isn't a big deal after all.

It takes forty-five minutes, during which time the courier arrives with a new phone and takes away the shattered one, for me to figure out what the emails are trying to tell me, what the emails have been hiding all along.

I stare down at the notepad where I've been scribbling details.

There's nowhere else to go from here.

But I'm going to bide my time. Making an unscheduled visit to Wilder Enterprises right now might upset the balance of everything.

And I don't want to run into Dominic.

I pick up the new phone, slip it into my purse, and then get my real phone from the bedroom.

Margo answers on the first ring.

"You'd better be calling to invite me to dinner, Miss Missing-In-Action."

"I *know.*" At least the sincerity in my voice, the sadness, is real. "I am. I'm starving and I want to see my best friend."

"Woah," she laughs. "Don't get too emotional, amiga. We've only been apart for a couple of weeks."

"It's too long," I cry, and Margo laughs harder.

"Sushi?"

"Perfect."

"Meet me outside your building in half an hour."

I hang up, strip off my clothes, and throw myself into the shower.

All the water in the world can't rinse away this piercing heartbreak, but it's all I've got...for now.

CHAPTER THIRTY-EIGHT

Dominic

CRAIG KNOWS SOMETHING IS UP AS SOON AS I GET INTO THE car, but one glance in the rearview mirror and he thinks better of asking what it is. I bark at him to take me to the penthouse.

Once I'm inside, I have no earthly fucking idea what to do with myself.

Over and over, I reach for my phone to message her, to call her back, to tell her that all of this was some kind of terrible mistake. That it happened because I'm tired. That it happened because I canceled my vacation and when I got back to the office some kind of crazy undercover shit storm was happening, and the FBI didn't want me to get involved in discovering who the culprit is. That the heat in the city gets to me when it's oppressive like this.

There are a thousand reasons for this to have happened, and all of them are stupid, senseless.

I'm in the penthouse ten minutes, pacing around and getting absolutely nowhere, before I text Craig to come back around.

"The club on Fifth."

He nods, and pulls away from the curb without another word.

It's the same club I took O'Connor too, and it's the only place I can think of in this godforsaken moment where I can be with other people and not be bothered.

My mind is still reeling when I step out of the Town Car into the evening glow. This is the kind of light that normally makes New York City look fucking romantic, but right now it makes my stomach turn. The dark interior of the club is where I need to be right now.

The woman behind the desk in the small lobby smiles at me, understated, not the overdone attitude of hostesses at the public restaurants. They're paid to be this way, paid to know the patrons but never reveal them to others unless specifically asked. "Good evening, Mr. Wilder. Would you like a private room, or will you be going to the lounge?"

Her question is a simple one, with a simple answer, and it's like a cold drink in the desert. "The lounge."

She dips her chin. "May I take your jacket?"

"No, that's fine."

Simple questions. Simple answers. The muscles in my back release some of the tension. Coming here is probably the first good idea I've had all day.

I follow the woman—Sarah, her name tag says, but I'm not convinced that any of the staff here use their real names to add another layer of secrecy, of exclusivity—into the lounge at the back of the building.

It could be any lounge, anywhere, and that's what I'm looking for right now—a place that could be anywhere, a place where I haven't just had a fight with the only woman to captivate me like this in my life and walked out on her.

I sit in one of the low chairs near a window, order a whiskey, and lean back, letting the hum of the conversation in the room wash over me.

There are maybe six other people in here. We're all in uniform, damn it, all in finely tailored suits, all obsessed with our money—you have to be, in order to be able to buy a membership here—and I laugh a little at that. Obsessed with our businesses, our money, and for what?

An image of my father flashes into my mind. *So you don't end up like him, that's why.*

The whiskey comes to the table and I drink more of it in one gulp than I should, then order a second. The burn settles me. The burn centers me. And finally, *finally,* my thoughts start to settle in.

I went too far with Vivienne, that much is clear, but I'm not sure if I went too far in being with her, or in the way I just conducted myself at her apartment. Probably both. But the more I drink, the more I look out the window and force myself to think about this like an adult instead of a paranoid child in a rage, the more I think I've done what I had to do to save Wilder Enterprises.

Not that she was putting my business in imminent danger of collapse—no. But somewhere along the line, this would have happened; somewhere along the line, it would have become untenable to keep letting her intoxicate me, letting her drown me in what we were becoming.

I can't even entertain the thought that what we were becoming was something damn incredible. I can't, and then I do, and it's like someone is punching me in the gut, reaching in through my rib cage and squeezing my heart with rough hands, squeezing it until it's about ready to burst.

I order another whiskey.

And then, because I can't think of any other damn thing to do, I pull out my phone and make a call.

Chris's voice is startled to say the least. "Dominic?"

"I'm calling *you* this time, old friend."

He hesitates. "Did you—what's going on, man?"

"Remember that exclusive club that you hated?"

"Yes..."

"I'm here right now, and I look fucking pathetic." I spit out the last two words a little too loudly, drawing the attention of some of the other people in the room. "Come drink with me." I signal to the waitress, who's already making a beeline to my table. When she's next to me, I cover the phone with my hand, like it makes any difference. "I changed my mind, sweetheart. I'm going to need a private room."

"Right this way, sir." Her eyes don't give away the fact that I'm making an absolute fool of myself. Part of me wonders if anyone in here recognizes me on sight, whether I'm acting out a self-fulfilling prophecy, ruining my reputation all by myself and dragging down Wilder Enterprises with me. "You must be hungry," she continues in her cool tone while I follow her unsteadily out of the lounge, down a hallway, down another hall to the right, and into a smaller private room, where she pours me a glass of ice water from a crystal pitcher. "Let me order you some appetizers."

"That sounds *wonderful*." The drinks are going to my head, to my heart, and it's not too late to pull out of this, but I can't do it by myself. "Chris, buddy—" I don't know who I am anymore. "Come to that club and ask for me in the lobby. It's time for a night out."

"Did something happen, Dominic?"

"You know what? I'll tell you. I'll tell you just as soon as you get here. Don't let me down!"

"I won't," he says, uncertainty ringing in his voice, and then the line goes dead.

CHAPTER THIRTY-NINE

Vivienne

ARGO TAKES ONE LOOK AT MY RED EYES, WHICH I'D convinced myself were well-covered with some artful and natural-looking makeup, and purses her lips. "You're a terrible liar."

Liar stings, even though she's saying I'm a bad one, and I can't help flinching. "I'm a *great* liar."

"What happened?"

"Nothing *happened.* Are we walking?"

"Not happening. You can try to change the subject all you want, but I'm not buying it." Margo cocks her head to the side, and her blonde hair, piled on top of her head in a bun that's somehow chic and messy at the same time, follows a moment later. "Did you get a boyfriend without telling me?"

I give her my best impression of being offended. "*What?* Why would you think I did *that?*"

"Because you're hiding crying eyes behind makeup, which means you've spent the last half an hour putting on fresh foundation, which you *never* do at this time of night."

Margo and I roomed together the first couple of years that I lived in New York City—right up until my work at the FBI demanded a solo space for when I was on undercover jobs. She knows me too well.

"It's not *night,* first of all. It's still light out. This could charitably be called *evening.*" I sigh. "But yes, I did...sort of get a boyfriend without telling you."

"Start walking," she says. "We'll talk at the same time, so you don't have to look at me."

"You're a good friend."

She rolls her eyes. "You could take a page from my book." Then she smiles at me, everything already forgiven. "So, who's the guy?"

"I can't tell you."

Margo cuts me a sideways glance. "Is this some forbidden FBI thing where you're not supposed to date your co-workers?"

"He's not technically a co-worker." Margo knows that I work for the FBI, but she doesn't know the details of the jobs I've been going on. My stomach turns over—neither does Dominic, which is why he's storming off across the city right now. "But that doesn't matter. What matters is, he was—I was *really* into him, and now it's over."

"You didn't cry this hard last time you broke up with a guy."

"I'm not crying *now*. I'm just walking to dinner."

"You didn't need fresh makeup, is all I'm saying." Margo takes a right, and I know which sushi place she's chosen—one of my favorites, without having to ask.

"Well—there's nothing I can do about it now."

"Nothing? You don't think it's worth a shot?"

The lie is on the tip of my tongue, but for some reason I can't bear to say it. "I don't know."

She takes a breath, frowning a little. "We don't have to come up with a plan to get him back right now. Give it an hour."

"There's not going to be any plan. I can't think of a plan." *I can't handle the thought that I could try with him, and he might walk out again...and I'm supposed to be stronger than that.*

"Give it a bottle of *wine*," she says, grinning, and *that* I can get on board with.

* * *

I'm thoroughly regretting the three bottles of plum wine we split between us while I ride the subway to Wilder Enterprises the next morning. That stuff is *deadly*—and it tastes so sweet that it's like you're hardly drinking alcohol at all, until you're very clearly drinking alcohol and you've had too much and your best friend has to walk with her arm looped through yours all the way back to your apartment so you don't take a tumble into the gutter.

I raise a hand to my eyes. What a shining moment.

My stomach lurches. I forced down an English muffin and some greasy scrambled eggs in an attempt to set myself straight before I had to leave for work. So far, it's failing miserably.

We never got around to plotting how I would win Dominic back, and it's a good thing, because it would have been frustrating for both of us to listen to me get cagey with the details. As Margo has said to me a hundred times, *the details make the plan.* She's usually referring to the outfits we're going to wear to a club or an art gallery opening. In this case, she's right—but I can't tell her what they are.

Not yet.

Not for a few years, anyway, and by the time I tell her, it will be far too late.

Another bolt of pain shoots right through my chest. Maybe I should go home, sleep this off, and—

No.

Dominic isn't going to take the day off, either. He'd never want anyone to think he had a weakness, that the weakness might be anything other than a deadly illness. He'll be in his office today, living and breathing above my head, and I'll just have to live with the pain. It's the only option I have.

My phone rings as I'm stepping out of the subway exit into

the golden morning sun, and I stifle the urge to heave on the sidewalk while I fumble for my phone.

The name on the Caller ID doesn't make me feel better.

"Good morning, Milton."

"We've got a problem." His terse tone sends a shock of cold into my gut.

"What is it?"

"You're out of time, Viv. I don't think you've got much longer before your cover is blown."

"I—what?" My mind reels. There's no way Dominic got in contact with anyone at the FBI about me—is there? Is that what's happening?

"One of the guys on the team—Chris O'Connor—says he met up with someone from Wilder Enterprises last night, and the guy has some pretty deep suspicions about you. From what O'Connor said, he doesn't have any solid proof, but my guess is that he'll be on the lookout for any reason to either fire you or expose you as an undercover agent."

We both know that can't be allowed to happen. "How much time?"

"Three days." Milton doesn't hesitate. "Three days, or we're pulling you, and we'll use an outside team to put this one to bed."

My heart sinks. I have most of the pieces I need to find this guy. It would have helped to have more than three days, but...

"It's not going to be a problem," I tell Milton, my thoughts racing ahead to the emails, to the plans I was going to put into motion over the next week. It'll all have to be expedited.

"If it is, we pull the plug. Fair warning."

Then Milton ends the call, and I'm on my own.

CHAPTER FORTY

Dominic

IT'S BEEN A LONG TIME SINCE I GOT SO OUT OF CONTROL, AND everything in my body rebels against it.

But not until it's way too late—not until I've been at Pendant for God knows how long, putting back drink after drink with Chris O'Connor, in the middle of the goddamn week.

When I wake up the next morning, my mouth is so dry I can barely swallow, and all my memories from last night are swimming in a thick haze of alcohol. Snippets from a conversation we had keep surfacing, but it seems so absurd that I can't believe I actually said any of those things, that Chris even answered.

"I know it has to be her, man." My tongue feels thick in my mouth, and drunk as I am I can still register, barely, how slurred the words are. *"There's just nobody else."*

Chris splits into copies of himself in front of me, the both of them pushing a glass of water toward me across the table. "Have a drink, Dominic. No!" He laughs as I reach for a glass of champagne. Whose idea was it to order champagne? That's a fucking drink for celebrations, not whatever the hell this is. "Water." He gets up, melding back into one person, and comes around the table to put the glass of ice water in my hand.

I sip at it. It's bitterly cold against the heat of my throat. "Tastes good. This is good water."

Chris sits down in a seat next to me. "You're not like this, buddy." His voice is soft, coaxing. "Let me take you home?"

"To what?" I slam the glass down on the surface of the table, too hard, and water sloshes over the rim. "There's nothing to go there for. My apartment is empty, damn it."

"Look." He seems like he's swaying, but I can't tell if it's me or him who's doing it. "You've got a shot with her. You can fix things. Tonight she was having a bad night. She'll get over it."

"Yeah, right. Yeah, right!" I shout the last word at the top of my lungs, and a strained smile plays over Chris's face. "People like Vivienne Davis don't get over anything. They never let anything go. That's what kind of woman she is. That's what kind, Chris."

His eyes have gone wide, but I have no idea why. "Vivienne Davis, huh?"

"You know her?" I reach for a drink and miss. "You know her, man?"

He presses his lips together like he's thinking hard. "It's not a name I've heard before."

"Well, if you knew her—" I lean toward him and almost fall forward off my chair. Chris puts out a hand and steadies me. "If you knew her, you wouldn't forget her, and now I have to live the rest of my damn life trying to forget her."

God.

I roll over and press my face back into my pillow. The room rocks around me, and it takes every bit of effort to reach over and silence the alarm that's like a jackhammer in my brain.

Get up and go to work.

My body ignores the command, slipping back into a still-drunk, half-hungover sleep.

* * *

It's not any better when I wake up the second time, but I have no choice except to get out of bed, because I'm not going to hurl on my sheets. I'm only willing to sink to a certain level.

After I empty my stomach, I stagger back to the bedroom and sit on the edge of my bed.

What a damn disaster.

My phone alerts me to the fact that it's nearing two o'clock in the afternoon, and that's the only thing that makes me stand up, trying to get my feet under me, trying to feel like I'm not still drunk. I'm not—there's no way I could be—but the world seems to sway gently around me.

A shower.

I need a hot shower.

Back in the bathroom, I turn on the water full blast and stand leaning against the wall, letting it run down over the back of my neck, for a long time. Then I reach for a bottle of shampoo.

Getting dressed and ready to go takes most of an hour. By the end of it, I'm feeling slightly less like I'm on the verge of death, but the thought of food is an abomination. Still, I go into the kitchen and force myself to drink half a bottle of water and choke down some buttered toast. I'm going to have to call someone in to cook tonight. I shouldn't go the entire day without eating, but standing at the counter makes me bone-tired.

When was the last time I did anything this stupid? It's been years, and the memory of it—especially in light of what I had to drink last night—isn't clear. Something in college, probably, because it wasn't long after that that Wilder Enterprises hit rock bottom and I dug it out with my bare hands.

Craig is waiting for me by the curb when I get downstairs. The eight steps from the door of the building to the car in the damp heat are torture, but I put one foot in front of the other until I'm situated in the back of the car, the air conditioning blasting down on the back of my neck.

When I look up, we still haven't moved, and Craig is staring at me in the rearview mirror.

"You sure you want to go to the office?" The question is as neutral as it can be. There's not the slightest hint of judgment in his tone. There's concern, nothing else, and it reminds me why I hired him in the first place.

"Yes. I'm getting a late start." The laugh that bubbles up from my throat is a horrible parody, and Craig looks at me for another long moment before he nods his head, going back to focusing on the traffic in the side mirrors.

What the fuck is happening to me?

As soon as the car begins to move, I'm overcome by a wave of what feels like the nastiest vertigo ever to have existed in a human body, and I have to put my hand out against the front seat and brace myself against the door to try to make it stop.

It doesn't work.

I'm falling apart, and it's because I gave up on Vivienne.

It's so crystal clear that the realization is blinding. I can't look at it head-on—not right now. I can't decide if it's true or just another hangover delusion. What I *do* know is that I can't go to work today.

"No," I rasp. "I can't—I have to go back inside."

We're barely three spots down from where we started, and Craig pulls smoothly back to the curb, then gets out and comes around to the passenger side door.

"Yeah, that's a good call. I'm going to take you back upstairs, okay?"

The only thing I have strength to do is to nod in agreement.

CHAPTER FORTY-ONE

Vivienne

I HAVE TO TAKE SEVERAL DEEP BREATHS BEFORE I CAN GET MY racing heart under control.

It's a gorgeous July morning, and at this hour of the day, the heat feels like a gentle warmth on my shoulders rather than an oppressive wet blanket. I'm wearing a sleeveless sheath dress, with a cardigan tucked into my purse in case I get chilled by the air conditioning at Wilder Enterprises, and I'm frozen on the sidewalk.

Get a grip, Vivienne.

I look out at the traffic gliding along the street next to me, the taxis coming and going, pulling smoothly up to the curb, gliding away, and take in another deep breath. The city *almost* smells fresh, and I step back against the building, glancing down at the awning covering the sidewalk in front of Wilder Enterprises.

In spite of everything, in spite of the raging hangover, the fight that happened because neither of us could just *cool down* for a minute, the fact that Dominic walked out on me and refused to talk to me on the phone and told me in no uncertain terms that it's *over,* I can't help but think of him stepping out of his Town Car and looking down at me in the rain. A man like Dominic has enough money and enough power to ignore a person on the sidewalk, but he didn't. He offered me his hand. He looked into my eyes, and he saw me, he *saw* me right then.

My throat tightens, aching in the same cadence as my heart, but I swallow it down. The mortifying fact of all of this is that I still want to finish out this investigation on a high note. I still want to find and help bring to justice the person who is selling energy technology secrets to a foreign entity. I want it for me—I want it for my career—but I still want it for Dominic, even after everything.

Maybe—*maybe*—if I can do this, then I can finally explain to him what all the secrecy was about, what he saw me hiding last night.

No—I can't do this.

I laugh out loud, on the verge of tears, and blink them back. What I *can't* do is stand out here on the sidewalk debating whether or not I can actually tell him the truth once this investigation is over. I don't have time for that. Anyway, it's all a moot point if I don't get a move on and blow this thing wide open on the tight schedule I've been handed.

I put a professional smile on my face and head toward Wilder Enterprises with my head held high, eyes glued to the traffic with every step, just in case Dominic crosses my path.

* * *

The first item on my agenda is to come up with a lie that will draw the person from tech support up to my desk. I don't have time to come up with a sophisticated plan, so I start by overloading the computer with every conceivable program I can open and then running the most complex tasks I can think of until the entire thing freezes up. Then I pick up the phone and dial down to the basement.

"Mark Sadler."

"This is Vivienne Davis," I start out, letting my voice shake a little. "I'm sorry to bother you guys, but there's something wrong with my computer and I just can't get it sorted out." I hate playing the damsel in distress, but sometimes it's the most effective thing.

"Okay. What floor are you calling from?"

This guy—Mark Sadler—could be the one. Based on what I've noticed in his emails, all signs point to him as a primary suspect. To prove my suspicions, I need access to his machine, and I don't have time to come up with a cute plan to stay after hours and then hope he's gone home for the day.

"Mr. Overhiser's office," I say, banking on the fact that he'll remember the names of the executives, at least. "I'm up here, and I just can't get this to work, and there's a *lot* I have to do—" I let my voice rise higher and higher in octave.

"Just hold tight, Ms. Davis. I'll be right up."

He clicks off the call and I do another performance of being frustrated in case anyone is watching from some hidden corner of the office, count to forty, and then I stand up, heading straight to the elevator.

My heart beats wildly. If he's on this car, right now, then it's going to look at least a little suspicious that I'm leaving and not staying to anxiously hover over his shoulder until the computer is fixed. I come up with several excuses—a last-minute drink order, being so overwhelmed by my emotions that I need to step outside, an urgent request to retrieve a file—and I'm prepared, but when the doors open, the elevator car is empty.

I take it down to the third floor, then let my eyes go wide for the benefit of anyone who might have noticed that I've never been here before, and step back in. I have to wait because the elevator is on its way to the upper levels, and when it gets back down there are two people inside—neither of whom are the tech support guy. Hopefully he's making his way to my computer right now.

I clutch the flash drive I'm going to need for his machine in my left hand and get back on the elevator.

When the doors open on the basement level, it's a different

scene from when I was here last. It's well-lit, and all but three of the offices have someone inside them, hunched over a keyboard. One of them swivels around as I make my way into the space. "Need something?" He's got red hair and dark eyes, and looks vaguely irritated to be interrupted.

"Just dropping something off," I say, holding up the flash drive and giving him my most charming smile. The corners of his mouth turn up, just slightly, and then he turns his back.

"Is it for the kid?"

Kid? I give a shrug, then continue on past the office.

Mark Sadler's office has his name on a bracket outside the door, and his computer is on, humming. I jam the flash drive into the first available port I see.

My heart is beating out of my chest, slamming against my rib cage so hard it's difficult to hear anything else. The drive needs thirty seconds to work, and that's probably how long I have before someone realizes I'm just *standing* in here.

Ten seconds.

Twenty.

Twenty-five.

Thirty.

The indicator on the flash drive blinks, and I grab it up as fast as I can.

But I'm not fast enough. I'm still standing up when Mark Sadler's voice interrupts me from the doorway.

"What are you doing?"

I slap a sheepish smile onto my face. "I thought—oh, this is stupid." I tuck the flash drive into my hand, hoping it's hidden from his view. "I thought I should come down and see you first. I'm just so impatient. But when I got down here I realized—"

He's not buying this.

"—that you'd already gone up."

"Okay..."

"But I'll get out of your way. How—how's the computer?"

"It's fine," he says, and there's something in his voice that sends a chill down my spine. He locks his eyes on mine. "Give me a call if you have any more trouble."

"Thank you *so* much," I gush, and I move quickly toward the door. He moves away from it, but a beat too late, like he might stop me. "I promise I won't bug you too much."

I can feel his eyes on me all the way back to the elevator.

CHAPTER FORTY-TWO

Dominic

I LOSE THE ENTIRE DAY ON WEDNESDAY TO FEELING LIKE SHIT, but when I wake up on Thursday, all the remaining alcohol and hangover bullshit has cleared itself from my system.

I'm a new man—all except for the dull ache at the pit of my gut. I try to ease it by ordering my chef to come in early and cook an enormous breakfast—bacon perfectly crisp, scrambled eggs fluffed to perfection, toast with a hint of cinnamon sugar—but it doesn't have much of an effect. Vivienne would like this breakfast, and every bite I take, I can't help picturing what she'd look like wearing one of my shirts, sitting across the table from me, enjoying the hell out of it after a night of—

I push those thoughts right out of my head. They're not going to do me any good now.

A full half-hour early, I call Craig to bring the car around. In comparison to yesterday, I feel unbelievably alive and ready to tackle the day, to make Wilder Enterprises the center of my life again.

Like it should be.

Even if my stomach turns over at the thought that a love affair with a company might be the best I can do, after Vivienne.

On the way into the office, I call an emergency meeting with my executive team. Half of them won't be in yet, but the ones who aren't will be rushing to get here as soon as they get my email. I start sorting through the messages from yesterday, firing off terse responses and generally reminding everyone that, yes, I am still in charge, despite yesterday's sudden disappearance. When Craig pulls up to the curb, just as I sign off on the last one marked "urgent," I square my shoulders. Not even Vivienne Davis is going to derail me.

Not for more than one day, anyway.

It feels like everyone in the lobby is staring at me, which can't possibly be the case, because large portions of the building are rented out to companies that have nothing to do with Wilder Enterprises and hence nothing to do with me.

It's not until I get to my office that I realize it's not some kind of delusion, because even Emily's expression seems off.

"Good morning, Emily."

She gets up from her seat behind her desk and picks a tray from her desk, her eyes lingering on me longer than usual. "Good morning, Mr. Wilder." She presses her lips together, watches me walk past her to my inner office, and then follows me in. "I hope—I hope you're feeling better this morning."

I take a seat behind my desk and look at her. "Do you want to tell me what's going on?"

Emily tries to give me a half innocent shrug, but she's clearly uncomfortable. "You were out sick yesterday, so I was—"

"You know what? It's fine." Something's up, and it's above Emily's pay grade, and grilling her on it like this is a dick move. If Vivienne walked in right now, she'd think—

No. *No.* I just got here. I can't let her consume me within the first five minutes.

But I can't help it. Vivienne trusted me, trusted me to take her places she'd never been before, and she trusted me to know when it was time for the power games she loved, and when it was time for us to be equals in bed. She'd expect the same kind of thoughtfulness everywhere else. She'd expect me to know when I was using my power against someone who didn't deserve it and refrain, for God's sake.

"It's fine," I repeat, and Emily's shoulders relax. She steps forward, setting the tray on my desk, and I make a determined effort to appreciate the sparkling water. "I'm sure you saw the email about the executive meeting."

"Yes." She nods firmly, obviously relieved to be back on solid ground. "I didn't put together an agenda—I assumed you'd want to lead the meeting yourself—but there's still time, if you'd like me to."

"No, I don't think this will take long enough for a formal agenda."

"Anything else, Mr. Wilder?"

"Not right now. Thank you, Emily."

I hear the little sigh she lets out as she crosses the threshold.

Fifteen minutes later, I'm striding into the meeting room down the hall from my office. Every pair of eyes turns to me, as they always do when I come into the room, but there's something strained in their expressions.

I close the door behind me with a click, then take my place at the head of the table. "Have a seat."

There's a general rustling as chairs are pulled out all around the table and people settle in.

"First item on the agenda," I begin, sitting casually in my chair like I'm completely at ease. "One of you is going to tell me what the hell has you all acting like I'm a glass figurine."

It's Childs, with his lazy drawl, who breaks the ringing silence with a little laugh. "Well, Mr. Wilder, we were all pretty concerned about you when the news broke yesterday."

"News?" A cold trickle of anxiety moves from my neck down my spine. What news is he talking about?

He must see the tension in my face, because he waves both hands in the air. "Gossip blogs. Some idiot with a camera saw you staggering out of your building yesterday afternoon and thought it was worth putting on the internet. Doesn't seem to have any major effect yet, but it's not like we're filing for an IPO." He laughs again—a risky move—but everyone else is stone-cold silent. "Did you stay out too late for the first time in a decade? What *was* that, son?"

It's so quiet I can hear everyone breathing, and I know a lot of shit hinges on this moment. The next several days hinge on this moment. The next several *weeks.*

So I laugh along with Childs. "You know what? That's exactly what I did." A few others around the table join in when they realize it's not a trick, I'm not goading them into anything. "I'm not a saint."

Childs lets his eyes go wide. "You're *not?*"

I give him a look paired with a half-smile, and everybody else laughs, too. I let them ride it out, and then, as it's settling, I put both hands on the table.

"Enough of this. Status updates, everybody. I want to get back on track, and I want to start right now."

They launch into their updates, and I settle back in my seat, trying to focus.

This might have been a narrowly avoided disaster, but it just proves that Vivienne wasn't the problem. Losing her was far more devastating.

Far more.

CHAPTER FORTY-THREE

Vivienne

I STAY UP ALL NIGHT WEDNESDAY NIGHT COMBING THROUGH the contents of the flash drive, and it's there.

It's *all* there.

A secret cache of emails that weren't being picked up by the original sweeps at Wilder Enterprises. A *separate* app, buried deep within the operating system, for transmitting the files themselves—encrypted, of course. Bank account information, payment transfers—*all* of it. It's the smoking gun. It's the proof that Mark Sadler is the one who's been selling the secrets.

I rub my hands over my face in the early hours of the morning, exhausted and energized at the same time. This is the proof Milton has been wanting me to come up with, and I can finally provide it. I can't actually *make* the arrests, because he wants a specialized team to do that, but I have all the evidence. Getting his computer will just be icing on the cake.

All I have to do is call it in.

But I hesitate reaching for the phone.

Milton won't give a shit that it's four in the morning, but there's a hollow pit in my stomach that doesn't feel anything like success.

The truth is that I can't do this without telling Dominic first.

Maybe it's because the two things—Wilder Enterprises and Dominic—have become so tightly intertwined in my mind that I can't end one of them without also getting closure with the other. I laugh out loud in my silent apartment. Closure in the sense that at least he'll know the truth about me. I don't know if closure about what we shared coming to an end will *ever* come.

Milton is going to need some time to call in the team, that's true, but I still have one more day remaining on his timeline.

"You have time," I tell myself out loud. My voice sounds ragged and tired.

I go into the bathroom to brush my teeth—my mouth is sickly sweet with the frappuccino I got from the all-night cafe down the street—and catch a glimpse of myself in the mirror. The bags under my eyes have reached epic proportions, and my skin is ghostly.

This is *not* how I want to approach Dominic to tell him. Not at all.

All at once, as I stare into my own eyes, all the fatigue from the last couple of days—the hangover, the sobbing, the all-nighter with the data—hits me, full force.

Four in the morning.

I can *maybe* get up at seven to make it to work on time, but just in case, I find my way back to my cell phone, dial Mr. Overhiser's office, and say that I need the morning off, I'm sorry for the short notice, something came up. Then I dial Stephanie's desk phone and ask her to cover for me, just for the morning—I'll be in shortly after lunch, I tell her.

It's a near thing, making it back to bed before I fall asleep, but I manage it, tumbling under the covers with my eyes already closed. As I drift off, an image floats to the front of my mind: Dominic smiling at me, shaking his head, forgiving me for this mess.

* * *

It's after one o'clock when I wake up, rubbing at my eyes, trying to get the world back into focus. When I see the time on my phone screen I bolt straight up in bed, my legs tangled in the sheets. "Shit. *Shit.*" It's *well* after lunch. "Way to screw up in the home stretch, Vivienne," I shout, while I run to the bathroom and fling myself into the shower. I'm already late, but I'm not about to show up at the office looking anything less than halfway perfect. Not today.

I rush through the shower but force myself to slow down. I twist my hair up behind my head so that I look like a lady and not a deranged animal who slept in too late and got doused with water. I take special care with my makeup, putting on some mascara and eyeliner, drawing it in with an oddly steady hand.

The first dress I pull out of my closet is perfect for—

What kind of occasion is this, anyway? Trying to get a meeting with my ex-boyfriend and former lover who is still technically my boss, although not *really,* because my real boss is Milton Jeffries of the FBI, so long as I can get this shit taken care of by the end of business tomorrow?

Regardless, it's a simple black sleeveless sheath with understated embroidery in a slightly lighter shade, summer flowers drawn with an air of professionalism. I slip into my heels, grab my purse and the flash drive, pop the second drive with a copy of everything I've found along with my summary and findings, and head out the door.

My skin glistens on the way to the subway. It's *hot,* and the sun is relentless. Just like it was when we went to that amusement park. My heart aches at the thought of Dominic popping cotton candy into his mouth and laughing. Everything before we got into the cab was the stuff that dreams are made of, damn it.

I'm rushing, but even so, Wilder Enterprises looms up before long, before I'm ready for this.

No choice. I have to be ready now.

The air conditioning in the lobby is a welcome relief.

First order of business is to go up to my desk and make sure Mr. Overhiser hasn't suffered a breakdown without me.

Naturally, he has not. He's preparing to go home for the day as I put my purse into the bottom drawer of my desk. "Hello, Mr. Overhiser," I call through his open door. "I'm sorry about this morning—I had—"

"It's not a problem, Vivienne!" he calls back. "I've got a meeting outside the office. I won't be back in." He pulls the last few of the things he needs from his desk, then closes all the drawers and comes out by my desk. "There are a few things that need taking care of," he says, glancing down at the stack of blue folders on my desk. Then he gives a little frown, like he doesn't *want* to have to assign me this work, but it's necessary. "By the end of the day, would you?"

I grit my teeth, putting on the biggest smile I can. I will *not* miss working for Overhiser when this is finished. "Absolutely."

Then he's on his way out the door, whistling as he goes, and my heart is in my throat.

It's time to call Dominic.

CHAPTER FORTY-FOUR

Dominic

"MR. WILDER—THERE'S AN UNSCHEDULED CALL FOR YOU. Can I take a message, or put it through?"

I turn away from my screen to where Emily is standing in the doorway to my office, one foot in and one foot out, ready to go back to her desk. "Who is it?" I finally have my balance again, after that bizarre executive meeting, and the afternoon is ticking away.

"Vivienne Davis, from the executive level."

The name makes my skin go hot and my stomach go cold. I don't want to talk to her—hearing her voice is going to be torture—but I'm the one who put myself in this position. I'm the one who pursued her. I'm the only one who can't fire her now.

At least it'll put me out of my misery. It won't take long to know whether she's over this already, the fight we had firmly in the past, or whether it's still an open wound for her, too.

I try to keep all of this off my face. "Put the call through."

My hands are slick while I wait for the indicator light on my phone to beep, and it does, an eternal moment later. I snatch up the handset too fast, too violently, and almost drop it.

Vivienne, I want to say, like we're both in bed together, like none of this happened, but instead I say, "This is Dominic Wilder."

There's the smallest sound over the phone line, like she's swallowing hard. "Mr. Wilder."

That's all it takes. That's all it takes, and I know with absolute certainty that this is killing her, just like it's killing me.

I don't know how we're ever going to get past this. I don't know how she could stay in her job—she'll have to transfer, at some point, because we can't—

"Is there something I can do for you, Ms. Davis?"

She takes another breath in, and then answers, the tension straining her voice. "I'd just like to meet with you for a few minutes, if you had some time this afternoon."

"This afternoon? No." I answer as quickly as I can, because it's true. I have meetings scheduled for the rest of the afternoon, and I'm not going to move them, as much as it's a knife in the gut for me to deny her anything, *anything.* My new focus has to be on Wilder Enterprises. I can't be having these kinds of conversations when I'm supposed to be building the company. Then another thought occurs to me. "Is this related to—personal or business matters?"

"Business." She says it steadily, but there's a little shake in her voice that tells me it's not entirely that, it will never be entirely that again.

"I'm fairly scheduled for the afternoon," I say, moving heaven and earth to keep my own voice in check. "Could you come by my office at about five-thirty?"

"That would be perfect. I'll see you then."

"Goodbye."

She hangs up before all the unsaid things between us can hang out there on the line, while we both writhe on the end of our hooks.

* * *

It's a damn miracle that I get anything else done for the rest of the afternoon. At ten to five, I go out to Emily's desk.

"Head out early today."

She stops typing and blinks up at me. "Are you—I've got a few more things to finish for—"

"Are any of them urgent and needed first thing in the morning?"

She considers, glancing at the screen. "No, I'm—I'm actually ahead of schedule a bit. These are for Monday."

"Head out early and enjoy the afternoon."

Emily gives me a smile and clicks out of the calendar. "Thanks, Mr. Wilder." She's gone within three minutes. The elevator doors slide open, then they're closing, and she's gone. I should give her early afternoons more often. She's never once complained about staying late.

I repeat the process for everyone else on the floor, and no one argues.

I can't sit still, so I pace over to the windows, then pace back, my heart revving up. Vivienne's not going to be late.

I'm right about that. The elevator doors open at exactly five-thirty, and there she is, walking past the empty offices and meeting rooms. Her eyes flicker from side to side, and as she gets closer, she presses her lips into a thin line.

She knows we're alone.

I go back behind my desk.

The air in the room is fiery with the tension, stretched tight, ready to snap, and Vivienne takes a big breath in, her green eyes huge, the color made brighter by the fact that they're red.

"Mr. Wilder." Her voice cuts the silence like a knife, and I can tell it's taking a huge effort to keep it in check. "I have—I have something I wanted to discuss with you."

"Take a seat." I do the same, sitting down in a parody of normalcy. "Go ahead, Ms. Davis."

She looks me squarely in the eye. "I don't want to dance around this."

"Don't."

"Okay." Another breath. "For the last couple of months, I've been working undercover at Wilder Enterprises. I'm an agent with the FBI, and I was sent here to determine if a member of your company has been selling sensitive energy technology information to someone affiliated with the Chinese government."

My heart thuds, once, twice, against my rib cage, and I can feel blood rushing to my face. I wasn't wrong, then. I was right, and she *was* hiding something from me.

"Last night," she continues, "I finally gathered the final pieces of evidence to prove that Mark Sadler, a member of your technical support department, has been doing just that." She reaches behind the folder she has pressed to her chest and produces a flash drive, which she drops on the desk between us, biting her lip.

Vivienne hasn't looked away from me, and she doesn't now, only her eyes are glistening, and the next breath she takes has a hitch in it. "I couldn't tell you, Dominic, and I shouldn't be telling you now. I should have called my boss early this morning so that they could put together a plan to make the arrest. But I couldn't—" Her voice breaks, and she swallows painfully. "I couldn't do this anymore. I couldn't keep hiding from you. I've been—I've been so heartbroken. I've been beside myself with the pain of not being able to tell you, of losing you, and I just couldn't—I couldn't do it anymore." She's still looking at me, tears streaming down her cheeks. "I couldn't do it. My job—it doesn't matter. I just— You don't have to forgive me."

For the first time, Vivienne looks down at my desk. "I have to make a call," she says after a moment of heavy silence. "I have to make that call, but I wanted to tell you first. I couldn't leave all this behind without telling you first."

Then she stands up, the back of her knees pressing her chair backward, and makes a move toward the door.

I'm out of my seat in an instant, around the desk in two steps, gathering her into my arms and kissing her hard, the heat escalating between us and around us and everywhere. Her tears are salty on her lips. The folder falls to the floor, and her arms go around my neck.

"No." My voice is husky, unstable. "Don't leave any of it behind. Don't leave. Come back to me."

CHAPTER FORTY-FIVE

Vivienne

DOMINIC'S VOICE IS A BALM ON THE SHATTERED MESS OF MY heart, and his words break me wide open, the silent tears turning to sobs of relief as he kisses me, again and again, his lips claiming me for his own, his need for me palpable in every single touch.

"I wanted to tell you," I say in broken phrases through the kisses. "I wanted—"

"I was a prick. I was fucking reckless with you, and I shouldn't have been." He pulls back, hands on my face, and stares into my eyes, his gaze piercing. "Vivienne, it all started coming apart from the moment I walked away from you. And I realized—I realized it was a bigger disaster to leave you behind than it ever was to stay with you." His voice is urgent, and I put my hands up on his wrists, holding on tight. "We can figure this out. Whatever it means for your job, for my company—we can figure it out. But I can't be without you. I *can't.*"

"I don't *ever* want to be without you," I say, with one final sob, and it turns into laughter at the tail end. "It was all so stupid, such a *stupid* fight—"

Then his mouth is on mine again, possessive and hot, and I melt under his hands. With one movement, he lifts me up and turns, backing me up until my ass makes contact with the hard mahogany of his desk, and with one sweep of his arm he clears it, an elegant pen holder and a desk calendar clattering to the ground.

His tongue explores my mouth like it's the first time we've ever kissed, and I can tell from his harsh breathing that he's barely able to keep himself in check. I feel the same wild energy and urgency pulsing through me, rocketing through me, and my clothes have never seemed like such an inconvenience in my damn life.

I wrap my hands around Dominic's neck as his hands move roughly downward, touching me like I want to be touched right now, touching me like I belong to him and I always will, and nothing will ever break us apart again. He shoves the skirt of my dress up around my hips and nudges his legs between mine so I'm spread out on the edge of his desk. With his lips on the side of my neck, trailing hot wet kisses down to my shoulder, he puts both hands on my panties and wrenches them down and off, tossing the fabric to the floor.

I hold on tight. I hold on like I'm drowning, like he's the last lifeline, and the sensation of his muscles moving under my hands as he undoes his buckle, unzips his pants, frees his hard and ready cock, is burned into my memory.

This isn't lovemaking, this is a hot, desperate fuck, and I'm soaking wet, spread wide, and Dominic doesn't waste a moment before he's thrusting into me, his hands on my ass, somehow keeping me steady on the edge of the desk.

"Yes...*yes...*"

He's buried to the hilt in one stroke, and all my muscles clench around him, my toes curling, all the pent-up energy focusing down to my molten core. "Never leave me again," he growls into my ear, and one, two, three thrusts and I'm over the top in my first orgasm, coming hard onto his steeled length, biting down on his shoulder to muffle my cries.

"I didn't leave," I gasp. "I didn't leave—"

His hands tighten on my ass, and he slows the pace for a few minutes, kissing the side of my temple, biting at my earlobe, his voice a low whisper. "You're right. I'll never turn my back on you again, sweet thing. Never again. You're mine."

"I'm yours."

The words ignite him again, and the languid pace evaporates in an instant.

"Tell me again."

"I'm yours—" I can hardly get a breath in, he's fucking me so hard, my legs spread to capacity on the desk, and my clit is throbbing with every stroke as our bodies make contact again and again, and I've been *dying* for this, I've been dying to be fucked, to be taken, to be possessed, and Dominic is giving it to me all in this moment, all in this hot, concentrated moment. The door to his office is wide open and he doesn't care, and I don't care, it's all I can do to even see past his shoulders.

My hair comes loose from its twist, spilling down over my shoulders, and with one hand still firmly on my ass, he reaches back and threads his fingers through it, pulling my head back, tipping my chin up so that my neck is exposed for him to lick in one long motion with his tongue.

"God, you taste so good—"

I tighten around him, completely unable to stop the moans escaping from my lips as I wind up again for another orgasm. When it hits, it's so powerful that I almost lose my grip on Dominic's shoulders, rocking dangerously into him, and he's holding me tighter than ever before when he goes over the edge into his own release, coming hard inside me with a sharp hiss.

We're locked in place, bodies trembling, for a long time after that.

Until Dominic lifts his head from my shoulder, sweeps my hair away from my face with his hands, and kisses me, tenderly, gently. "I love you, Vivienne Davis."

I make a face, and he pulls back another few inches. "What?"

"My name *is* Vivienne."

He gives me a wry grin. "Is this the last of the secrets, then?"

"I swear. My name is Vivienne Peterson."

"I can live with that." Dominic purses his lips. "Unless you want to take my name when—"

I burst into laughter. "You are *not* proposing to me right now."

He looks hurt. "Why not?" Then he grins. "When I *actually* propose, it won't be in my office."

"Why not?" I echo, pretending to take in the space for the first time. "It's *so* romantic."

He helps me off the desk, helps to straighten my dress, tugging it back into place before he zips his pants, threading his belt back into an appropriate state. "We *did* meet in front of this very building."

I roll my eyes. "That was—not one of my more shining moments. So maybe we just agree to forget it?"

He laughs out loud, and I shift my weight to the side, getting ready to head to the door. We don't need to be here anymore. I need to make a call, and Dominic—

My heart drops straight into my toes, ice cascading through my veins.

Because Mark Sadler is standing in the doorway, face pale, both hands wrapped around a Beretta 92, the black gun trembling slightly in his grasp.

CHAPTER FORTY-SIX

Dominic

VIVIENNE'S FACE GOES PALE, AND THE EASY LAUGHTER tumbling out of my mouth turns into a silence.

"I'm not going to let this happen."

The voice behind me is totally unfamiliar. I don't think I've ever heard it before in my life. I'm torn between a desperate need to see who the hell this is, and what the hell they're talking about, and the need to stay looking at Vivienne.

She presses her lips into a thin line, then reaches slowly for my arm, pressing her hand against my elbow so that I turn. "Slowly," she whispers. "Slowly."

I turn around, and my heart jumps.

Security hasn't been a big issue at Wilder Enterprises. Many of the firms who rent space from us hire their own security, and

I have a team stationed outside the building, but I've never been one for a militaristic presence in the front lobby. The regular team that assigns visitor badges has always done a fine job, but with a plummeting sensation I realize, too late, that I should have done *something* once O'Connor clued me in on the investigation. I should have been able to foresee this kind of situation—

My thoughts go silent when Vivienne's voice breaks in.

"What are you talking about, Mark?" Her tone is even, casual, with just a hint of confusion. "You should put down the gun."

"I'm not putting down the *gun*." Mark speaks the words through a clenched jaw. His sandy hair looks like he's been running his hands through it, and his shirt is soaked with sweat. "And you know what I'm talking about. You know *perfectly fucking well* what I'm talking about."

"I really don't, Mark." Vivienne is slowly shifting her weight, moving ever so slightly toward me, in front of me, and I resist the urge to throw my arm out to stop her. I am *not* going to let her take a bullet for me, FBI or not.

"You've been after me. You came to my office, and you did something to my computer, and it's over, okay? You're not doing that anymore." His eyes are wide, the color almost swallowed up by the whites of his eyes, and he glances between me and Vivienne like it's a tic he can't control. "I can't let you do this."

Vivienne raises her hands in the air. "I'm not doing anything. I'm just—having a conversation with my boss."

"I don't care if he's your boss. I don't care who you're working for, the Feds, or—" He swallows hard. "I don't care. This ends now."

"I don't understand." Vivienne lowers her arms, spreading her hands in what seems like a plea for explanation. "What are you hoping to gain from shooting us?"

She's moving again, almost like she's become frightened, slipping her hand behind me but keeping her back straight. There's the softest sound of plastic brushing plastic, like she's lifting the handset off the phone, and her fingers whisper over the keypad.

"What are you doing?" Mark's voice is loud, rough, and Vivienne flinches like she's been hit, jumping back into her place.

"I just want to know why you're planning to shoot us, Mark. Or is that not your plan? Are you planning to do something else?" She raises her shoulders, drops them down. "Look, if you're looking for a conversation, we can sit down and talk. All you have to do is put down the gun."

The gun shakes in his hands, the barrel bobbing up and down. "It's too late for that."

"It's never too late to talk. You can start talking right now, if that's what you came here for."

"I didn't have a choice!" He shouts the words, almost spits them, at Vivienne. "I didn't have a choice, okay?" Then his mouth twitches into a grimace. "Why couldn't you just stay the fuck out of it? I know you did something to my computer. I know you've been after me."

I can't stay silent anymore. "Mark, I own this company, and I can assure you that I never sent anyone to—"

"Shut your mouth." The barrel of the gun swings toward me, and I can feel every thudding heartbeat in my throat. I don't have a trick to pull with the phone, and I sent everyone home. *I sent everyone home.* "I've seen her in my office twice now, trying to fuck with my computer."

"If you haven't done anything," Vivienne cuts in, "then what do you have to be worried about?" Her tone is just as level as always. "Mark, I think something else is going on here. I think maybe you're in over your head with a situation you don't feel you can talk about, and you're making rash decisions."

"A *situation*—" Mark laughs bitterly. "You don't know what it takes to—you have no idea how expensive—"

"Tell us, Mark," Vivienne says, and the concern sounds genuine. "Whatever it is, you can tell us. Look, I think I know what you've been doing. But you don't have to make it worse, okay? You don't have to take it this far. We can talk this out. We can find a way to—"

"No!" Mark screams the word, his voice choked with rage and desperation, and right then, he breaks.

Time comes to a halt, and I watch the barrel of his gun bob, then swing back toward Vivienne. He's hesitating, but he's going to do something, his finger tense around the trigger, and I *see* it happen when he takes the first shot.

I throw my arm out to push Vivienne to the floor, to get her out of the way—I don't care if this man, this deranged man, kills me, but Vivienne, no I can't let her—but she's not there. She's rushing forward, putting herself between me and Mark, and the bullet doesn't come. The bullet doesn't come because it hits her in the side.

And she keeps going.

She keeps going, even when the bullet rocks her backward, she keeps rushing forward and she *gets there,* her hand coming down hard on his wrist. He lets go of it with a cry of pain, and then it's in her hands.

"Jeffries, get them in here!" She shouts it at the top of her lungs while she turns the gun in her hands and levels it at Mark. "Don't move, Mark. Don't move at all. Put your hands up."

"Vivienne—"

"Dominic, just stay where you are—"

I don't know who she's shouting at, but the next moment, there are five agents bursting out of the stairwell and from the elevator, racing down the hall, and they converge on Mark, pinning him.

Vivienne kneels down, hand on her side, and puts the gun gently on the carpet, and then she tumbles to her side.

I get there just in time to cushion the blow.

CHAPTER FORTY-SEVEN

Vivienne

THE BEEPING IS WHAT WAKES ME UP.

At first, it filters into the dream I'm having. I'm dreaming that Dominic and I are at an amusement park, only it's a vast, sprawling thing with hundreds of booths and attractions, with paths winding between them in such a labyrinth that it's impossible to find our way. He's totally unconcerned, laughing in the sunlight, his sleeves pushed up to his elbows, top buttons undone, his dark hair lifting gently in the breeze. "We can agree to forget this, Vivienne," he says, his voice warmer than the sun.

"I don't want to forget it," I tell him. "I'm trying to remember where we saw the ice cream."

"You're sweet like ice cream," he says, putting his arm around my waist.

"We saw that before." I point to a booth I'm sure we've seen before, only it keeps changing while I try to fix my gaze on it.

"I'll buy you all the ice cream you could ever want."

"Cotton candy," I say, and I can taste it on my tongue, the sweetness, the sugar, and Dominic laughs again.

The beeping starts again, a steady tone. "What is that?"

"What is what, sweet thing?" His voice sounds strangely like an echo, and I put my hands to my ears. It feels colder, but the sun is still out, still drenching the entire amusement park. I shiver.

"Vivienne?"

"What is that?" I ask it again, but my mouth doesn't seem to work as well this time. The amusement park starts to lose all its color, the vivid brightness leaching out of it, the beeping growing louder and more annoying, and for an instant everything goes dark.

Then my head breaks the surface and I open my eyes to see Dominic's blue eyes wide in front of mine, looking at me with such concern and love and hope that my heart shatters all over again.

"*Vivienne*," he says.

I can't help but smile at him. My lips are dry, and my eyes feel gummy. When I raise a hand to rub at them, I discover for the first time the hep lock in the back of my hand. "Hi."

"Hi, sweet thing." Dominic reaches for my other hand, takes it in his, and raises it to his lips. "Hi."

I blink, once, twice, and there's a nurse leaning over him, too.

"How are you feeling, Ms. Peterson?"

"I—" Wasn't I going by Davis? I narrow my eyes, trying to make sense of all this. "My side hurts."

"That's a side effect of getting shot," she says, her voice smooth and low. Her hands are working at the gown I'm wearing, and my side throbs again. Shot? The memories filter up from somewhere deep in my mind. Dominic's office. Mark Sadler. The flash drive. I start to bolt upright, and the nurse puts a hand on my shoulder and presses me gently back down into the pillows. "Calm down, honey. Did the pain get worse?"

She's peering into the side of my gown, but the dressing there must meet her satisfaction, because she deftly ties the strings closed again. "The flash drive." My voice is a little rough.

Dominic squeezes my hand. "They took it off my desk. They have everything they need."

"There was a second one, but it was—"

"They got that, too. Your boss was harassing me about where your purse was just about the second you got out of surgery."

"Did you tell him?"

He rolls his eyes. "I told him it was probably in your desk, and then I told him where the desk was. He started to suggest that I *show* them where the desk was, but—" Dominic laughs. "I've been here with you every moment. What an absurd thing to ask."

I crack a smile. "That's Milton." He'd want all that stuff collected as soon as it was appropriate—sooner, if he could get away with it—and it looks like they did. "Did they—did he say—"

"He said you did a fantastic job." The nurse steps away and turns down the volume of the machine that's beeping.

"I'm going to go get you some food, Ms. Peterson," she says. "Some food and water. Call if you need anything in the meantime." Her eyes travel over Dominic, and the corner of her mouth quirks in a smile. "I doubt you will, though."

I give her a nod, and she disappears out the doorway.

Dominic raises my hand to his lips again, eyes locked on mine, and his next breath comes along with a ragged hitch. "You scared the shit out of me, Vivienne Davis—Peterson." He grins at his own correction. "I was ready to be the hero."

"You *were* a hero."

"I was not. I let you get shot."

"No." The memory is getting clearer by the second. "You tried to save me." I smile at him, my heart aching with joy that he's still here, still with me. "I was just busy doing my job, that was all."

"Vivienne." My name is like a prayer on his lips.

"Dominic."

"I love you."

My eyes fill up with tears in an instant. "I love *you*."

"I'm never going to leave your side again."

I laugh. "I hope you leave my side *sometimes*. Otherwise, it could be a little oppressive."

"Fine, fine...you can go to work. But first, we're going on a vacation."

"A vacation?"

"As soon as you're out of the hospital, we're heading out. And we're not coming back for a month. Maybe longer."

I can't believe what he's saying. His last vacation went down in flames in less than a week—there's no way he'd take a month off from Wilder Enterprises.

"You can't do that."

"I can do whatever I want. And what I want is to take you somewhere warm and gorgeous and spend every moment with you, showing you that you mean so much more to me than a company ever could."

I have to pick my jaw up off the floor. "Dominic, I don't—I don't know if *I* can take a vacation for that long."

He gives me a look. "I already cleared it with your boss."

"Wow." I try to look stern. "That's pretty presumptive."

He leans in close, his eyes shining. "No, it's not."

I breathe him in, the scent of him filling me with warmth and hope and love. "No, it's not."

Then his lips are on mine, and the rest of the world fades away. Nothing else matters. Nothing else ever will. Not like this.

CHAPTER FORTY-EIGHT

Dominic

VIVIENNE LOOKS RADIANT IN A PINK SUNDRESS, HER HAIR loose and curled down her back. It's her first day out of the hospital, and I brought her back to my penthouse the moment we could escape. I watched her face light up at the racks full of vacation clothes, at the suitcases waiting to be packed, at the hair and makeup team I hired to make sure she feels like a damn princess every single moment.

She looked up at me with a shy smile. "I'm a little pale and sickly for this kind of thing, don't you think?"

"Not at all."

That was the last of her arguments, and she willingly went into their hands, emerging from the spare bedroom-turned-dressing room after two hours freshly showered, her hair blown out and curled to perfection, and her face glowing.

She'd come to me in that pink sundress, bare feet padding on the carpet, and put her arms around my waist, giving me a tender hug. "Thank you." Then she'd taken a deep breath. "You smell good."

"I spent some time getting ready, too."

I took her hands in mine and held them over my heart. "Tell me the truth."

Vivienne's brow furrowed. "About what?"

"Are you too tired to leave today? You can be honest with me. We can delay as long as you need to."

She'd looked around the penthouse. "You're telling me your private plane doesn't have a bedroom if I need to rest?"

"It does, but—"

"Dominic Wilder, I have been in a hospital room for too long, looking at the same four walls. And before *that*, I was spending all my time at various desks at your office building." She gave me a look. "Don't get me wrong. You have great taste in office furnishings. But I am ready to be somewhere else. With you."

"You don't want to overdo it." The concern crept into my voice in spite of myself.

"I'm very nearly healed," she said, putting her arms around my neck. "And you can help me out of this dress any time and see for yourself." She raised her chin and kissed me on the neck, then the jawline, then took my earlobe between her teeth for a fleeting second. "I'd prefer if you did it on the *plane*, though, and not here."

"This is a perfectly good penthouse." My cock was already pressing hard against the zipper of my pants.

"But your *plane* can take us somewhere exotic. Far away from here."

"You're right."

I put my hands on the sides of her face and pulled her in for a kiss that started out soft and sweet and almost immediately turned into something hotter.

"Dominic!" She pushed me away, laughing. "All these people—"

She gestured at the people moving in and out of the spare bedroom, carrying suitcases and makeup kits and pushing portable mirrors and lights. Most of them were trying not to watch us, but a few of the women had indulgent smiles on their faces.

"You're right. It's not fair to them." I took her hand in mine and smiled down at her. "Let's go."

Now, forty minutes later, we're just waiting for them to finish the final checks on my jet. Vivienne stands in a tucked-away waiting area in the terminal. It won't be long until we're ready to walk out on the tarmac, climb into the plane, and jet off together. First stop, the Bahamas. Second stop...anywhere.

My phone buzzes in my pocket, and I pull it out absentmindedly, only to feel my heart pick up when I recognize the number on the caller ID.

"Are you okay here for a minute?" I murmur into my gorgeous

girlfriend's ear.

She nods, not looking at me. "More than fine." She's watching the activity around the plane with rapt attention, but then she turns and beams up at me. "I'm so *excited.*"

I kiss her temple and turn away, swiping to answer the call as I head out into the main hallway.

"Dad?"

"Dominic, it's me." My dad's voice is gravelly, but familiar. It's been a long time since we talked.

"I know, Dad." Pain spikes through my chest, along with a strange compassion. "What can I do for you?"

"Well—" He breathes in, then lets it out slowly. "I saw on the news that something happened at your building, and I wanted to make sure you were okay."

My building. He used to call it *his* building. For years after he almost lost it, it was still his. Now it's mine.

"I'm fine. I had—I had some good luck." It's a huge understatement, but it's what I've got.

"That's good, son. That's very good."

Something cracks open in me then, and I can't stop the words from pouring out of my mouth, words I've never said to him before. "Dad, I have to ask you something."

"Ask." His tone is a little astonished. I haven't spoken to him like this in years.

"I don't—" Now that we're here, I don't know how to say it. "I don't get it, Dad. I don't get how you let Wilder Enterprises get so out of control. I've met someone and I thought—Jesus, I thought that meeting her was a disaster because it would take my mind away from the business. But I realized—shit happened, and I realized that she's the only good reason to focus on it, to grow it, to make sure nothing happens. If she ever ended up like Mom—" This is an awful blow, and I know it.

"There's something you should know, Dominic, and I don't think I've ever had a chance to explain." My dad's voice is tight with relief, with caution, with everything he's never said. "I took all that time off because your mother—she was desperately unhappy. I didn't know what else to do, so I tried everything."

It's dawning on me now, bright as day, and with a plummeting sensation, I realize what a dumbass I've been.

"I tried everything—the vacations, the trips, the hobbies—because I thought it might make her happy." My dad sighs heavily. "It wasn't enough." He swallows hard. "I didn't mean to let you down, son. I was just trying to fix things with her first, and then I was going to get back to business. I should have found—found a balance."

"No, Dad." I have to speak around the lump that's risen in my throat. "No. I'm—this was my mistake. This was my misunderstanding. If anything like that was happening to Vivienne—"

"Vivienne is a gorgeous name," he says softly, and I take the olive branch in both hands.

"*She's* gorgeous." I'm overcome by a flush of love and warmth in my chest. "Vivienne is gorgeous, Dad. She's gorgeous, just like

Mom." It's in this moment—right now—that I finally understand how much my father loved my mother, and why he moved heaven and earth for her, regardless of how those actions affected less consequential things like Wilder Enterprises. Because that's how I feel about Vivienne. My dad loved my mom more than anything. Understanding and appreciation stream through my veins, through my soul, for my dad, and everything he gave up for my mother. It's nothing less than I would give up for Vivienne.

"Listen—come see me when you have a free minute, okay? I'd—like to meet Vivienne."

"We'll be back in a month. You'll be the first stop." I take in one more breath. "I'd love for you to meet her, too."

There's a weighty pause. "Enjoy your vacation, Dominic. I—I love you."

"I love you, too, Dad."

I hang up the call and let the significance of all of it sweep through me. How could I not have seen what was really going on?

A hand on my arm brings me back out of the storm. It's Vivienne, looking up at me with her deep green eyes, a cautious smile playing over her lips. "They're ready," she says softly. "Are you okay?"

"I'm good. But I'll tell you more about it on the plane, if you want." I wrap my arm around her, pulling her close and breathing her in. "After—"

"After what?"

"I show you the bedroom."

She grins up at me, then takes my hand in hers, lacing our fingers together, and pulls me toward the door, out into the sunlight, and my entire body feels light and warm and free.

EPILOGUE

Vivienne

W E'VE BEEN IN THE BAHAMAS A WEEK WHEN I COME SLOWLY out of a deep, delicious sleep in the middle of the night. Dominic's hands are on me, gently stroking my face, and I turn into his touch.

"Mmm."

"Vivienne, wake up." His whisper is excited. I want to know why.

I blink a few times, my eyes adjusting to the darkness of the room. We're sleeping in a giant king-sized bed with pure white sheets, a four-poster with flowing fabric covering all four sides, and Dominic is sitting on the edge of the bed, a lit candle in his hand.

"What's going on?"

"I want to show you something."

"What?"

"I'll *show* you." He grins in the darkness, and I can see the outline of his white teeth against the backdrop of his newly tan skin.

I slip out of the bed, pulling on the light silk robe I keep hanging on one of the posts, and dart into the bathroom to brush my teeth. When I come back out two minutes later, Dominic is standing near the double doors that open directly onto a white sand beach. The ocean waves lap gently over the shore, the sound becoming more of a background noise every day that we're here.

"Come and see this."

He opens the doors and goes out onto the sand, wearing a pair of linen pants and a dark t-shirt that hugs his muscled body. I step out behind him.

And gasp.

The beach is covered with candles—hundreds of them, maybe thousands.

"Oh, my God." I cover my mouth with my hand. "Dominic, what is this?"

"It's magic, isn't it?" He reaches back and takes my hand, leading me down a path in the middle of the candles, toward the shore.

He takes his time, stepping carefully, fingers moving against mine with every step, and as we walk, a soft violin pipes up from somewhere near our little beach house. It's so pure, so vibrant, that I suck in another breath, turning to see who the musician is. She's a shadow against the white of the building. After a few moments, another one joins in. My heart aches to bursting. It's that gorgeous.

We make our way down to the shore, to the last dry spot before the waves, and Dominic looks out over the water. It's a brilliant night, warm, with a thousand stars above us and a thousand candles on the shore below. I'm caught in the starlight. I'm swept away.

Then he turns to face me. "Vivienne Peterson," he says, and the tears are spilling out of my eyes already, I can't stop them, I don't care to stop them. "From the first moment I saw you, I knew you'd stay in my heart and my mind forever. I'm just lucky that you've stayed in my life." He bends down to one knee, pulling a small box out of his pocket. "I hope I can stay by your side for the rest of time." He opens the box, and the ring inside glints in the flickering light. "Will you be my wife?"

"Yes!" The answer bursts out of me almost before he's done speaking, and he stands, sweeping me into his arms, kissing me hard and hot and furiously, then pulling back, laughing, to put the ring on my finger. The violin music swells, then melts back into silence.

Dominic wraps me in his arms, and I'm laughing with joy, surrounded by light and hope and beauty.

"*That* was me proposing," he says into my hair.

"That's the beginning of our lives," I answer.

His only reply is a kiss.

For more books by Amelia Wilde, visit her online at awilderomance.com.

Made in the USA
San Bernardino, CA
25 July 2019